THE CEREBRATED JUMPING FROG OF CALAVERAS III
Martha Dodson and Robert L. Forward

For the transformation they wanted, a lot more than a princess's kiss was needed!

THE SLOW-DEATH CORRIDOR
Mark J. McGarry

The half-living corpses produced vital medication—but were they only *half* alive?

A GIFT OF SPACE
Margaret C. Hewitt

Her dedication to her work and its standards was absolute—why did she betray them?

GRANDFATHER CLAUSE
L. Neil Smith

A paradox is a paradox is a paradox . . .

Also edited by Judy-Lynn del Rey:

STELLAR #1

STELLAR SCIENCE-FICTION STORIES #2

STELLAR SCIENCE-FICTION STORIES #3

STELLAR SCIENCE-FICTION STORIES #4

STELLAR SCIENCE-FICTION STORIES #5

STELLAR SHORT NOVELS

A Note about the Cover: Though the painting that adorns this book was inspired by Robert Zend's poem "5980 A.D." (see page 1), artist Jon Lomberg retains his own personal interpretation: "The beautiful, glowing nebulae we admire so much are often the sites of star formation. As the cold, dark gas and dust of the galaxy are compressed by shock waves, they form stars. If you come back and look at the Horsehead Nebula in a million years time (or if you're traveling so close to light-speed that 10^6 years star-time = 1 hour ship-time), you will find that the nebula has given way to hot, young stars. When these stars live out their lifetimes and die, they will again become cold, dark gas and dust. In that sense our Universe of Stars *is* a chess game between Black (cold, dark high-entropy material) and White (hot, bright low-entropy material). Is Gravity alone the hand that moves them? Or is there Something(one) Else? I don't claim to know. I do know that a pithier expression of the laws of thermodynamics (in an open universe at least) is this: Black wins. In a closed universe, the game might get played over and over endlessly, but with a different set of rules each time.

Stellar*6
SCIENCE-FICTION STORIES

EDITED BY
Judy-Lynn del Rey

A Del Rey Book

BALLANTINE BOOKS • NEW YORK

In memory of my dear, dear mother
NORMA BENJAMIN
(June 30, 1919–June 27, 1979)
And to the future of her glorious granddaughter
ALYSSA NORMA BENJAMIN
(November 14, 1979)

A Del Rey Book
Published by Ballantine Books

Library of Congress Catalog Card Number: 80-68216

ISBN 0-345-28969-2

Manufactured in the United States of America

First Edition: January 1981

Contents

5980 A.D.

dashing through space
  with nearly the speed of light,
    his moments—centuries,
      his weight as that of a planet,
        the cosmonaut saw the black
          Horsehead Nebula taken, and
          replaced by a white Bishop:
            he rubbed his eyes in disbelief,
              but when, from beyond,
                a slow and thundering
                  voice,
                    ricocheting from star to star,
                      echoing among galaxies,
                      said:
          "IT'S YOUR TURN, BLACK!"
                he realized that the universe
                    was a chessgame between two gods
                              —Robert Zend

Till Death Us Do Part

James P. Hogan

The apartment looked out from high above London's fashionable Knightsbridge, across Hyde Park toward where the green sea of treetops washed against white cliffs of elegant Park Lane buildings that had not changed appreciably in the last hundred years. Spacious, light and airy, and opulently draped and furnished in contemporary style, the residence was not the kind that came with the income of the average Londoner of 2056; but then the four people whom Harry Stone had come from Las Vegas to meet there that morning were hardly average Londoners, and their income was what he had come all that way to talk about.

For tax purposes the apartment was owned by a nebulous entity registered as *Zephyr Enterprises Limited*, and described as a business property retained for the use and entertainment of clients and customers visiting the capital. The company rented it for ten months of the year at a nominal sum to Nigel Philiman and his wife Delia, who, it turned out, happened to be managing director and company secretary respectively of the holding company that had set up Zephyr. To comply with the minimum required by law, the Philimans spent two months of each year abroad or elsewhere while the apartment was being used by clients. The clients often turned out to be friends who needed somewhere to stay while mixing a considerable amount of pleasure with a modicum of business in the course of a visit to the city, but that was purely coincidental.

3

Nigel was in his late forties, suave, athletic, sun-tanned and silver-haired, and always immaculately groomed and dressed. Delia was only a few years younger, but she had a countess's bearing and a movie star's looks, and knew just how to choose slinky, body-clinging clothes that enhanced the latter without detracting from the former. The couple went well with the apartment's image of luxury and high living, and Harry Stone was well aware that the image was no mere hollow sham.

Where their money came from was none of Harry Stone's business. Being a professional he had done some discreet checking on the side, however, and he knew that Zephyr had obscure links to a string of loan companies that seemed to specialize in financing such operations as escort agencies, various types of modeling agencies, an employment agency that hired waitresses and hostesses, and home or hotel visiting massage services—in short, anything to do with girls. The girls employed by such enterprises always worked according to a strict code of ethics written into their contracts, and they accepted payment only in the form of checks or credit cards that could be verified by accredited auditors. But like any man of the world, Harry knew that the girls were seldom averse to cultivating friendships further in their own free time, and that any additional such transactions were strictly cash. Where a portion of that cash might wind up and how it might get there were interesting questions.

Clive Philiman, Nigel's younger brother by ten years or perhaps slightly more, ran a group of agencies that specialized in handling rented apartments on the west side of London. Out of curiosity Harry had purchased a selection of the kinds of magazine that younger, single women tended to read, and had found a number of Clive's companies taking prominent advertising space in several of them. He could imagine that Clive, with his dark-brown eyes, classically Roman features, tight curls of short black hair, and sympathetic manner, might be just the kind of person that a girl just in from the country and looking for somewhere to live might find easy to talk to, especially when she learned that he just happened to have the right contacts to give her a job. And of course, making money might become her main problem when she discovered that the great bargain which had brought her into the office had been rented just an hour before she showed up.

Barbara Philiman, Clive's slim and petite, auburn-haired wife, had a good as well as a pretty head on her shoulders; she was director of a personnel selection agency off Wigmore Street which procured managers and senior executives for a wide spectrum of companies and corporations ranging from manufacturers of plastic labels to builders of space stations. This position gave her numerous social contacts throughout the capital's commercial world, and, Harry thought, were she so inclined, she would be the ideal person for somebody who perhaps was interested in arranging some entertainment for an important visitor to know. Furthermore, the agency would have been able to supply a tax-deductible invoice to cover the costs of screening a lot of nonexistent job applicants for positions that had proved unsuitable. It was just a thought.

All Harry Stone knew officially was that the Philiman family wished to convert a substantial inflow of cash from sources they chose not to disclose into a legitimate form of income the British Inland Revenue would be obliged to accept—despite any suspicions they might harbor—as justifying a life-style built around diamonds, personal flymobiles, à la mode gowns from Paris, and jetliners chartered for mid-Atlantic orgies thinly disguised as parties. In the capacity of financial and legal consultant, he had spent the morning explaining how he thought an American institution known as *Neighbors in Need*, with which he happened to have "personal connections," might be able to help solve their problem. Essentially, the organization managed the investment of large sums of money collected by charities of one kind or another, and distributed the proceeds among various worthy causes it was pledged to support. This service was rendered in return for a moderate commission on the amounts handled, plus expenses. Harry's proposition involved setting up a British chapter of the operation.

The British subsidiary would be guaranteed to attract a massive response to the quite moderate program of advertising Harry had outlined. The response—mainly in the form of anonymous donations—was guaranteed because the so-called donations would be almost completely made up of the Philimans' own hot money mailed to themselves after conversion into money orders and travelers' checks bought with cash all over the country. The packages would be opened and the contents registered by certified accountants, thus providing unimpeachable proof of where every penny of the chapter's assets had originated.

"Twenty percent stays here for salaries and expenses, which is the maximum allowed under British law," he said when he summed up the main points. He was speaking easily and confidently as he sat in an armchair of padded purple and chrome that looked as if it belonged in some eccentric millionaire's sculpture collection. The rings on his fingers glittered in the sunshine streaming through the window as he made an empty gesture in the air. "The remaining eighty is tax exempt and goes to the States as your gross contribution to the fund. Obviously you're all charitable-minded people, and there's no reason why you shouldn't add in a personal donation of your own or some deductible contributions from your companies' profits. Four times a year they pay you back a commission that they list as foreign expenses, which brings your effective total revenue back up to fifty percent; you pay tax on only three-fifths—that is to say, the thirty that's fed back. The remaining fifty covers the actual input to the fund, the parent company's commission, and U.S. domestic expenses. I guess that's about it." He sat back in his chair, steepled his fingers below his chin, and studied the four faces before him.

Nigel, looking relaxed in the chair opposite, took a

measured sip from the glass of sherry in his hand and savored the taste with an approving nod before replying. "You're still talking about a full half of it," he said. His voice was calm, registering curiosity rather than surprise or indignation. "Allowing for the portion that's taxable over here, we'd end up with the minor share. That does seem rather overambitious, wouldn't you agree?"

Harry knew Nigel knew better than that. He spread his arms expressively. "Most of their half has to go through to the fund. It's a respectable fund management operation, and it's got its payments to make. The rest helps them make a living, something we all have to do."

"What percentage goes into the fund net at the end of it all?" Barbara asked from where she was sitting on the sofa to one side, next to Clive.

"What I've described is the deal," Harry replied evenly, avoiding a direct answer. "They're not asking where the donations would be coming from at this end."

"It's still a big chunk whichever way you look at it," Clive said. He rubbed his nose dubiously, then looked across at his brother. "The money's clean on their side from the moment it enters the country," he pointed out. "We run all the risks over here. That's a difference that should be reflected in the split. I'm for this scheme in principle, but not for settling up as it stands."

"Your money is also hot, and that's another side to the same difference," Harry countered smoothly. "It's unspendable, and therefore might as well not be there. Half a loaf is better than no loaf. Your risk is balanced out by their doing you a favor that you need, which squares things back at fifty-fifty."

A short silence fell. Delia walked back from the window from where she had been listening and stopped behind Nigel's chair. "I presume, Mr. Stone, that this matter would be subject to a written contract confirming all these figures and terms," she said, speaking in a precise English society accent that was marred only by a slight tendency toward being shrill.

Harry's brow furrowed into a pained look. "Of course," he told her. "Everything would be legal and aboveboard. They wouldn't do it any other way. They've got a valuable reputation to protect."

Nigel sniffed pointedly, but made no comment. Harry smiled to himself and marveled at the mental gymnastics that enabled somebody in Nigel's position to be capable of a gesture implying moral disapproval. Although the bargaining had been tough in places, his instinct made him confident the deal would go through. The Philimans had politely but firmly argued him down from his opening proposal of seventy-five / twenty-five, which he hadn't expected them to accept for a moment, and declined his original suggestion of a one-year-deferred commission, which would have given the U.S. side of the organization the exclusive benefit of a substantial sum accrued as interest. But the negotiations had all been very gentlemanly and a refreshing change from the kind Harry was used to. Furthermore, everybody would be able to have dinner in a civilized manner afterward with all business matters forgotten.

Harry admired and envied the ability of these people to keep different parts of their lives in the proper compartments, and the tradition that enabled them to smile apologetically while they twisted the knife in deeper for the last ounce of flesh. This was the way of life he meant to become part of before much longer, and he recognized in the present situation not only the prospect of some lucrative business but also an opportunity for some social investment that could pay handsome dividends later. Anybody who was just smart could make money, but to really fly high in the circles that mattered, you needed something extra that people like this had. Harry Stone knew that he had it too, and he was going to prove it.

Nigel kept his face expressionless as he turned toward Clive with an almost imperceptible raising of his eyebrows. Harry could feel a warm surge of jubilation inside as he read the signals, but kept his own face just as straight. Clive's jaw stiffened a fraction, his eyebrows dropped, and he moved his head in a slight sideways motion.

"Sixty-forty," Nigel said, looking back at Stone.

It was what Harry had been expecting, but he frowned intently at the floor in front of him and went through the motions of wrestling with figures in his head. "It's scraping the bone," he said dubiously when he finally looked up. "But since we're talking pretty big dollars, I'd be prepared to try them for another three points. I'm sure we'd be wasting our time if I pushed for anything past that."

"Not enough," Nigel said flatly. "Make it another two. We'll meet you at fifty-five."

That gave Harry forty-five, which clinched the deal because his bottom limit had been forty-three. Nevertheless, he played through some more mental agonies and then asked guardedly, "Would we have a deal if I managed to get them to go for that? No more strings. You'll okay a contract if they beam it through later today?"

Nigel looked over at his partners, and one by one they returned faint nods. "Very well, Mr. Stone," he agreed. "You have a deal. Provided that the terms are as discussed and that our lawyer finds nothing amiss with the details, you may consider the matter settled."

Harry waited for a couple of seconds and then nodded. "I'll see what I can do," he said. "I'll probably be able to call you later this afternoon. Will you be at home?"

"Until about six," Nigel told him. He looked around him to invite any final comments, but there were none. "Very well, we'll consider the subject closed until I hear further from you." The Englishman set his empty glass down and braced his arms along the side of his chair. "There was another matter that you wished to finalize today, I believe," he said.

Stone nodded and reached inside the jacket pocket of his suit for an envelope containing a bank check for forty thousand pounds. He had purchased it two days before in Las Vegas with unlaundered cash bought at a substantial discount, and arranged for it to be wired on to London for collection on his way to the Philimans' apartment that morning. "One hundred thousand dollars, less twenty percent for handling as agreed," he said as he leaned forward to hand the envelope to Nigel. "It gives me a much better break than the standard rate. We're throwing it in as a goodwill gesture."

"*We?*" Nigel looked mildly surprised. "I thought you said this was a private matter."

"A figure of speech," Harry told him with a grin. "Okay, *I'm* throwing it in as a goodwill gesture. I think you'll find everything in order."

Nigel opened the envelope and took out the check, examined it briefly, and nodded. "Excuse me for a moment, please," he said, and with that got up and left the room.

Clive stood up from the sofa and brought his arms up level with his shoulders to stretch gratefully, his action echoing the more relaxed atmosphere that had descended to mark the end of the day's primary business. "It's a beautiful day for seeing some of London if you're not intending to return straight away," he remarked, glancing across at the window. "The weather must be the best we've had so far this year."

"I am staying over tonight, but I've got other things to do," Harry said. "I'll have to schedule that in for some other time."

"Perhaps you would care to join us for lunch," Delia suggested. "A new French restaurant has opened in the plaza downstairs. I'm told the cuisine is excellent."

Harry turned his hand palm upward and smiled regretfully. "I'd love to, but I only got in from Vegas this morning and it's a full day. I promise I'll allow for it next time."

"You must live a very busy life," Barbara murmured, leaning forward on the sofa and looking at him with a hint of intrigue that he felt she was not in the habit of displaying toward everyone. He was flattered, and he wondered for a moment if the look in her eyes might be an oblique invitation to get in touch sometime when his schedule was less crowded.

"Always busy, but never too busy," he said, winking in a way he knew could be read as not completely play-ful and pretending not to notice Clive's stiffening pos-ture out of the corner of his eye. "You know how it is with Americans—work hard, but play hard too, huh? Who needs ulcers?"

"I presume you travel Arabee," Clive said in a voice cooler than before. Though speaking to Harry, he glanced down at Barbara pointedly. "There were some things I was hoping to discuss, but I don't think this would be a good time. Could we fix something for a day next week, perhaps?"

Harry realized he had been getting carried away. "Yes," he replied, dropping his smile and producing a pocket vipad from his jacket as he turned to look up at Clive. He activated the unit and studied the information that appeared on its miniature screen. "Sure, I've got some free slots next week. When do you want to make it?"

"Before Thursday," Delia said, looking at Clive. "Don't forget we're due for a long weekend with Mau-rice and Brigitte in Cannes."

Clive took his own unit from his shirt pocket, com-pared his schedule with Harry's, and eventually they settled for a Tuesday morning meeting to be followed by lunch. They had just finished dictating the details into the two vipads when Nigel returned with a flat leather briefcase. He set it down on the side table next to Harry, then opened it to reveal bundles of used one-hundred-pound notes.

"Fifty thousand," Nigel announced, at the same time handing Harry a white envelope he had been carrying. "Here is the promissory note and some ID that you will have no trouble with."

Harry checked the contents of the envelope and then leaned over the table to spend the next minute or two counting the cash. His canceled bank check plus a copy

of the promissory note from Zephyr Enterprises to re-
pay the "loan" would satisfy the British authorities that
forty thousand pounds had been invested in the company from legitimate sources. Thus through the two
transactions that he had made in two days, Harry had
converted fifty thousand dollars he had borrowed on a
short-term basis into the equivalent of one hundred
thousand dollars in illicitly obtained cash. That left him
with the problem of translating the profit into personal
assets that couldn't be questioned, but he would take
advantage of his visit to London as an opportunity to
solve that.

At last he pronounced himself satisfied, closed the
briefcase, and exchanged final farewells as he stood up
to leave. Nigel and Clive began talking about some office space that was available in Piccadilly, leaving Delia
and Barbara to escort Harry to the door. Just as she
was about to close the door behind him, Barbara said in
a low voice, "It might be fun to find out what you're
really like, Harry."

"I'm planning on moving over permanently not long
from now," he murmured. "Maybe when I do, I'll give
you a call at the office. I still need somebody to show
me this city."

"Do that," she whispered, smiled a promise, then
eased the door shut. Harry tightened his grip on the
briefcase and began whistling jubilantly through his
teeth as he turned and walked in the direction of the
elevators.

The first thing he did after he came out of the main
entrance to the apartments was call the States and arrange for a contract to be beamed through to Nigel Philiman in accordance with the terms agreed. The terms
were immediately accepted as Harry knew they would
be, but not wanting to give the impression that things
had been too easy, he postponed calling Nigel back until later. After that he had a snack lunch consisting of
an unchilled beer and a ham sandwich in a pub at the

top end of Sloane Street, and then took an autocab eastward toward the center of the city.

He found the premises of Melvin & Cooper, Dealers in Rare Stamps, Coins, and Curios, in a side street off Charing Cross Road. It was one of those quaint old London establishments that had barred windows guarding its displays and solid brasswork its portal, and gave off the impression of having stood there since the street was first laid down way back in whatever century and of boasting the same venerable and dignified staff that had unlocked the doors on its opening day. Inside, Harry spent almost another hour discussing and examining postage stamps, eventually selecting a modest collection dating back twenty years. The complete purchase came to just short of fifty thousand pounds, and Harry paid in cash. The dealer dutifully recorded the details of the transaction and the date along with the name and address of the buyer, the latter of which he took from the document that Nigel Philiman had provided.

From there he took a cab to Marble Arch, where he locked the briefcase containing the collection in a bank deposit box rented for twenty-four hours under his assumed name, after which he called Nigel as promised and advised him that, after a lot of haggling and effort, he had persuaded his associates in the States to go with the figures that Nigel had asked for. That issue having been resolved satisfactorily, he spent thirty minutes in a corner house unwinding and congratulating himself over a cigarette and coffee. It had been a good day's work, and the time was three-thirty, just right for him to get to Bayswater by four to meet Sandra. Now business was really over, and for the rest of the evening, not to mention the night, he would be able to abandon himself totally and with unashamed selfishness.

As he drained the last of his coffee he paused to check back over the day's events for any last detail he might have forgotten. Then, finding nothing, he stubbed his cigarette, smiled to himself in satisfaction, rose from the table, paid the bill, and left.

* * *

Feeling ecstatically content, Harry Stone lay back against the silky softness of the pillows admiring the rear view of Sandra's perfect body as she stooped provocatively in front of the vanity to straighten her hair in the mirror. "Wow!" he murmured approvingly.

Sandra smiled over her shoulder in the mirror. "Feeling better?"

"Fantastic! If this is only the beginning, hey, are we gonna have some good times. I never went much for that crap about people being made for each other, but you know something—it's true."

"You, a romantic? I'd never have believed it." Sandra smirked wickedly. "I'm starting to get hungry, Alex. How about eating dinner early? Then maybe we could go on to a club for a couple of hours and still have plenty of night left. I have to be away early in the morning."

"Oh, how come?"

"I promised I'd go to an art show with a couple of the girls from the health club I told you about."

"The place with all the loaded man-hungry widows and debutantes on the prowl for rich husbands?"

"Uh-huh."

Harry shrugged. "Sounds good to me . . . especially the last part. We could go to that place in the park again by the bridge."

"Great." Sandra moved over to the door and slipped on a robe she took off a peg on the back. "I need to shower," she said. "Don't run away, Alex." She left the room, leaving the door open behind her, and disappeared into the bathroom in the hallway. The sounds of cabinet doors being opened and closed and bottles being set down trickled back into the bedroom. Harry stretched out an arm to pick up his cigarettes and lighter from the bedside table, lit one, tossed the pack and lighter down again, and settled back to relax.

There was nothing especially remarkable about bumping into a fellow American overseas, but to have decided for no particular reason to have lunch in the same restaurant as this American three months before had been a rare and unexpected stroke of good fortune, even for somebody like Harry, who made it his business to be lucky. Sandra had come to England three years ago as the wife of a vice-president of a Texas-based construction company who had moved over temporarily to set up a British division of the firm. Her husband had become infatuated with an English girl and taken her back to the States with him at the end of his stay after offering Sandra a generous settlement in return for an easy divorce. Since then she had continued living a life of ease and leisure in London, cultivating the circle of social acquaintances that her husband's position had brought her into contact with, but always managing to be free when "Alex" was due to stay in town.

But what he liked most was that she was the same kind of person as he—a born winner. She knew what she wanted and played hard for it, and acknowledged the fact realistically without hiding behind apologies or pretense. Without doubt she was his kind of woman. They both understood the rules of the game and would play it together for as long as they both had something to gain; if that ever changed, then that would be it, with no dues, debts, or recriminations either way. So nothing was guaranteed but his prospects were looking pretty good, and all the signs indicated that when Harry finally moved over to London as planned, he'd have everything set up and waiting for him. Success, in all its aspects, had never smelled sweeter.

The sounds of shower water were replaced by the low hum of the hot-air dryer system. "When are you going back home to Surrey, Alex?" Sandra called through the doorway.

"Not until later tomorrow," he replied, making his tone not very enthusiastic. "I'll let myself out if you have to get away. I've got to see a couple of guys from a broker's in the city, but not until around lunchtime."

"Which ones are those—the Australian nickel or the Brazilian coffee beans?"

"Something different. We tied up both those deals this morning," he told her.

"So how many millions was that worth?"

"Oh, you know how it is," he drawled carelessly. "A couple here and a couple there. I figure the commission on it should take care of the dinner check tonight."

"So what is it? Tell me."

"Ocean ridge mining. A new treaty's been drafted by the UN that's pretty well bound to go through. It's the right time to be taking out options."

A short pause ensued. Then Sandra remarked in a more sober tone, "You didn't sound too happy about going home tomorrow. Is she being a bitch again?"

Harry scowled and blew a stream of smoke across the bed. "Yes, but I don't want to talk about it. Why spoil a nice evening? Anyhow, it's not as if it was going to be for much longer."

The hum of the dryer stopped, and Sandra reappeared through the doorway, her robe on again. For the first time that afternoon her expression was serious and her manner tense. "You are still sure you want to go through with it?" she said. "You haven't changed your mind?"

Harry hesitated for just a second, then nodded once decisively. "I don't change my mind," he told her, stubbing the butt of his cigarette in the ashtray by the bed and looking up. "Did you get the . . . *things*?"

"Do you really want to talk about that now?" she asked. "Why not leave it until we get back?"

He shook his head. "Let's get it over with and out of the way now. Then we'll be able to enjoy dinner without it hanging around in the background . . ." He grinned crookedly. "Not to mention afterward."

Sandra nodded and, keeping her face cool and expressionless, walked over to the wall closet. She slid open the door and reached up to the shelf inside for a padded brown mailer. She drew out a small white package, replaced the mailer on the shelf, and came over and sat down on the edge of the bed. Harry watched as she opened the white package to reveal a pre-formed plastic container—flat and about two inches square—of the kind used for holding one-shot medical infusers. She flipped the lid open with her thumbnail and uncovered slender metal tubes lying side by side in three of the container's slots, the remaining two slots being empty. Each tube was a little longer and slightly thicker than a match, and was tipped by a glass bead at one end. Two of them had a tiny dot of red paint on the outside about halfway along; the third was plain. Sandra selected the plain one and lifted it from the container. She handled it delicately but surely, her movements telegraphing a cool determination that Harry found momentarily chilling.

"Anyone would think you're unwrapping candy or something," he murmured. "Doesn't this bother you at all?"

"Objective thinking," she said, glancing up at him from under her long, curling eyelashes. "It doesn't have to be like this, Alex. You could always walk out and get a divorce. I thought *you* wanted it this way."

Harry inhaled deeply and was surprised to feel his breath coming shakily. "And get screwed out of every penny I'm worth to keep her in Scotch and hippie boyfriends who don't have the brains to earn their own suppers?" The sound of the bitterness in his own voice steeled his resolve; he nodded curtly. "Yes, I do want it this way. Come on, explain it again and show me how this thing works."

Sandra held up the tiny tube she had taken from the plastic container. "This is a standard medical infuser for injecting drugs as an atomized jet straight through the skin," she said. Harry nodded. Though he was not on any course of medication that required their use, he knew about them, since such devices were not uncommon. Sandra indicated the container in her other hand. "Those other two, with the dots on, are not filled with anything prescribed by any doctor. They're a special kind you can get if you know the right people, and they contain a volatile nerve toxin that's lethal within seconds of becoming active. You'd use one of them like this." She put the container with the two "special" infusers in it down on the bedside table and pulled a cigarette out of the pack lying beside it. Then she snapped the glass bead off the end of the tube she was still holding and touched it lightly against the side of the cigarette just below the end. Nothing happened for about a second, and then the tube began emitting a faint hissing sound. As soon as the hiss started, Sandra drew the tube smoothly and slowly along the length of the cigarette, timing her movement such that it just reached the filter as the sound died. "It takes four or five seconds," she told him. "Make sure you get rid of the glass tip. A few people are doing long stretches because they got careless over that."

Harry took the cigarette from her fingers and examined it curiously. There was nothing on its surface to indicate anything abnormal. Actually he did know about "squirts," as the lethal brand of infusers were called in the underworld, which was where they were usually procured. In fact he could have obtained some himself from Max or Tony or a couple of his other less salubrious acquaintances in Vegas; but there had been no point in risking leaving a trail that might lead back to him there, where he was known, especially not after Sandra had suggested such a solution independently and offered to obtain the stuff for him. But too much familiarity with such matters would not have gone with the image of Alexander Moorfield, commodity broker and investment banker from Maryland, currently living in Surrey, England, so he pretended to be fascinated and just a little nervous.

"That's all you have to do," Sandra said, watching his face. "Then there'll be no alimony to worry about, and you'll be able to afford some nice flowers out of the life insurance."

"Wouldn't I taste anything funny when I smoked it?" he asked, looking up at her with a mild frown that was fitting to his role.

Sandra shook her head. "The poison enters the bloodstream through the lungs and doesn't become active until after about half a day," she said. "Then, when it reaches a certain center in the brain, it works almost immediately. It's quite painless. You get hit by a sudden feeling of tiredness that lasts maybe a couple of seconds, and then it's all over. The molecules break down into residues that are indistinguishable from waste toxins produced naturally in the body, so there's no way that anything could show up in an autopsy."

"What about the butt?" Harry asked. "Wouldn't a lab be able to find traces in that?"

"That's possible, but you'd have to be really unlucky," Sandra replied. "Just remember to clean out all the ashtrays before anybody has a chance to think about getting suspicious."

He met her eyes for a second. They were calm and unwavering, and seemed to be challenging him to prove he was everything he said he was by not backing down at the last minute. He drew a long breath to give the impression of a respectable citizen bracing himself to take an irrevocable plunge and found that the nervousness he tried to feign was coming naturally. "Okay," he said from somewhere down in the back of his throat. "It looks simple enough."

Sandra closed the plastic container and returned it to the white package, then took it across the room to the closet and slipped it into a jacket pocket of his suit. When she came back to the bedside table, she picked up the glass bead, the empty infuser, and the cigarette that she had treated, and carried them through to the kitchen where she dropped the lot into the garbage incinerator.

"Where the hell did you get those?" Harry asked as she came back into the bedroom.

"You don't really expect me to answer that," she said reproachfully. Her manner was becoming more teasing now that they had the worst of that particular subject out of the way. "Let's just say I've got friends, and they're not all pillars of virtuous society."

"Did you have to go to bed with someone?" he asked. His voice was matter-of-fact, but his eyes were studying hers curiously as he spoke.

"If I did, would it bother you?"

"Aw, come on . . ." Harry spread his hands appealingly. "We're both grown-up people. If that's what you have to do, it's what you have to do."

Sandra hesitated for a split second, then said, "Yes, I did."

With her chin raised a fraction, she was looking at him defiantly. Harry had the feeling that her answer was meant to test his reaction. "Hey, stop glaring at me as if that's supposed to cut any ice," he told her. "I've been around too much for that." He lay back against the pillows and grinned. "Anyhow, what's new? I already knew you were a bitch. That's why we're right for each other. Boy, are we gonna go places together when all this is over!"

"So when will that be?" Sandra asked, moving a step nearer. "Have you worked something out yet?"

Harry nodded. "I've got a business meeting scheduled at one of the banks in town for Tuesday morning," he said. "I'll take care of it sometime just before I leave. That'll give her all day with me out of the way, and I could see you here in the afternoon to celebrate."

"And after that, are you still planning on selling up the house in Surrey and moving into town?" He detected a trace of disappointment in her voice. "It sounds such a nice place."

"Hell, I wouldn't want you in there," Harry said, pulling a face. "I could use a break in town for a while. After that—aw, there are plenty of nice places."

Sandra nodded in resignation. "How long do you think it'll take?"

"Who knows?" Harry spread his palms. "But there's no reason why I couldn't move out right away—the end of next week, maybe. So if you owe any outstanding payments on those little babies, you'd better get 'em cleared up pretty quick."

Sandra brought her hands up to her hips and stared

down at him accusingly. "You really are a bastard," she told him. "You don't give a damn how I got them, do you."

Harry clasped his hands behind his head and grinned up at her. "You said I shouldn't ask about that, and I believe you. Anyhow, now tell me you don't like bastards."

"Mmm . . . maybe there are one or two around that I could find time for," she said, breaking into a smile.

Sandra had been gone for a few hours by the time Harry emerged from the apartment late the next morning, the white package zipped securely in an inside pocket of his jacket. He went to Marble Arch and retrieved the briefcase from the deposit box, added the package to its contents, and then took the briefcase to a store in Edgware Road that handled a variety of lines including packaging materials. For a small fee one of the assistants boxed and wrapped the briefcase in a manner suitable for mailing, and Harry then took the parcel to the Marble Arch post office, where he consigned it to himself under a box number in Las Vegas. After that he walked half a block along Oxford Street and into the central London branch of Remote-Activated Biovehicles (U.K.), Limited.

The girl at the reception desk greeted him with a warm smile of recognition. "Good morning," she said. "Was your trip enjoyable?"

"Very enjoyable, thanks," Harry told her. "I need another reservation for Tuesday. Any problems?"

"The same model?" the girl inquired, activating the computer terminal beside her.

"Oh, yes. It's very important."

The girl scanned quickly down the table of information that appeared on the screen and began tapping a string of commands into the touchpad with deft motions of her fingers. "No problem," she announced brightly. "The reservation is made, and you can pick up the confirmation in Las Vegas." She looked up from the screen. "Are there any problems to report?"

"Maybe a few minor scratches and blemishes," Harry said with a wry grin. "Nothing that some rest and a high-protein transfusion won't cure by tomorrow. You might get some complaints about a few aches and pains if you let it out again today, though."

The girl smiled knowingly. "We'll take care of that, Mr. Stone. I'll put it down for a full checkup, regeneration, and recuperation." She entered some more instructions into the terminal. "Will you require the same accessories on Tuesday or will there be any changes?" she inquired.

Harry thought for a second. "Maybe a thinner suit now that the weather's warming up. How about a light blue with a fine silver pinstripe? I'll leave the matching of the necktie, cuff links and tie clip to you."

"Jewelry, wallet, cigarette lighter, pocket vipad, and cash?" she asked.

"Fine as they are. Make the cash five hundred pounds, one hundred of it in tens."

"Is there any cash to be credited to the account?"

"It's not worth the messing around. I'll lock it up and pick it up again on Tuesday."

"As you wish." The girl completed her operations at the terminal and smiled over at him again. "If you'd like to go on through, cubicle number six is free. We'll see you again on Tuesday, Mr. Stone."

"Take care."

Harry walked through a door at the back of the reception foyer and into a corridor flanked by a dozen or so doors on either side, all bearing numbers. He entered the one numbered "6" and found himself in a small, cheerfully decorated and warm room that contained little apart from a comfortable leather-upholstered recliner and a small table upon which was an open metal strongbox. He emptied the contents of his wallet onto the table, added the personal items from his pockets, and then placed them all in the box, after which he closed the lid and scrambled the combination lock. Just as he was finishing, a knock sounded on the door and an attendant in a light brown tunic entered.

"Good morning, sir," he said cheerfully. "Lovely day for traveling. Is everything ready?"

Harry pushed the strongbox across the table toward him. "Hi, we're all set. This is for the vault."

"Anything to be forwarded on?"

"No, that's it."

"Very good, sir." The attendant produced a vipad from a pocket of his tunic and activated it to display the format of a standard R.A.B. (U.K.) Ltd. deposit-box receipt already filled in with details that the girl had entered at the reception desk outside. He added the identification number of the strongbox in the space provided and passed the vipad to Harry, who verified the transaction by tapping in a memorized personal code. The attendant took back the vipad, picked up the box, and left the room. Harry made one last check of his pockets and person, then sat down in the recliner and allowed his body to sink back into its soft, enveloping contours.

"Everything is ready, Mr. Stone," a pleasant voice said after a few seconds from a concealed speaker above the door. "Are you ready to leave?"

"All set," Harry murmured absently.

"Thank you. Have a good day."

The helmet that had been covering his head all the way around and down to the level of his chin slid smoothly away and retracted to its storage position above and behind him. He opened his eyes and lay waiting in the darkness. After a few seconds the lighting came on and increased to a low level revealing details of another small cubicle, this one including the usual wall of panels and electronics that he had never understood. He blinked a couple of times, then sat up slowly and sat for a moment on the edge of the couch to give his lungs and circulation time to adjust back to a normal level of activity. Then he stood up carefully, did his best to smooth two days' worth of creases from the open-necked shirt and casual slacks that he was wearing, and moved toward the door. He felt cold and a little bit stiff, but that was nothing abnormal.

The first thing he did in the corridor outside was visit the men's room, always first on the list of priorities after coming back. He emerged five minutes later and walked out the door at the end of the corridor that led through to the desk.

The young man at the desk had been expecting him. "Hello, Mr. Stone," he said. "How was London?"

"Just fine. It's been cold there, but it's getting warmer. Do you have my charge made up?"

"Right here." The clerk pivoted a flatscreen display around to face Harry, who ran a cursory eye down the details of the account, then verified the charge with his personal code. "And you have another reservation in London for next Tuesday morning." The clerk handed across a white plastic document holder. Harry checked the details, grunted, closed the document holder, and slipped it into the back pocket of his slacks. Then he bade the clerk good day, walked out of the front entrance of the Las Vegas branch office of R.A.B. Inc., and went to have an early-morning breakfast at the all-night restaurant a short walk up the street.

All Harry really knew was that you walked into a cubicle in Las Vegas or somewhere, they put a thing on your head, and a few seconds later you were walking out of another cubicle in London or wherever inside another body that was yours for the duration of the trip.

Somebody had explained to him once that the bodies rented out at the far end were not legally classified as people because they were grown under the control of synthetically manufactured DNA, designed to produce a physical human form complete with all the lower brain functions that took care of subconscious monitoring and regulating of respiration, circulation and the like, but with no cerebral cortex or any of the higher faculties the law decreed to be essential ingredients of personality. The unused part of the skull contained instead a microelectronics package that collected the information coming in through the nervous system and transmitted it to the nearest R.A.B. office, from where it was relayed across the world by satellite and somehow injected into your brain by the thing they put on your head in a way that shut out the input from your own body. Also, the signals from your brain to control voluntary movements and so forth were short-circuited off from your own body and transmitted back in the reverse direction. So you could see, hear, feel, and move around by remote-controlling a body that was five thousand miles away while your own self stayed in Las Vegas. Harry wasn't sure of the details, but traveling now took no time at all, and it sure beat the hell out of being jammed into tin cans for hours on end and having to fight to airports and back again. It was expensive, especially if you went for the deluxe models that came with best quality clothing and accessories, but the business community found it a much better investment than physically shipping executives around the world on short visits and having to handle all the accompanying problems.

Remote-Activated Biovehicles, or R.A.B., had the lion's share of the world market and was referred to popularly as "RentABody," or more frequently, "Arabee." Breakdowns in the system were rare but did happen occasionally, in which case an Arabee walking around somewhere would usually tense up suddenly and keel over. The company had an efficient system for dispatching recovery teams swiftly to deal with such emergencies, and the public had come to accept an Arabee crash as just another part of living that they might have the privilege of witnessing and being amused by one day. In fact there had been a few unfortunate instances in the early days when a case of genuine illness had received less than prompt attention because somebody had misinterpreted the situation. Since then the company had installed warning systems that activated automatically in the event of a malfunction to enable anyone who happened to be nearby to recognize the true nature of the event. All in all the system worked well and proved popular, and problems were few.

Harry never relished the prospect of having to return to the particular brand of domestic bliss that came from being married to Lisa, so he had announced that he wouldn't be back from New York until late that night, intending to spend the day in town. However, his mind had enjoyed little rest, even if his body had been immobile, and he realized over breakfast that he was sleepy. Thus he changed his plans and steeled himself to the dismal thought of confronting his wife early in the morning. So dismissing fond memories of London from his mind for the time being, he took an elevator up to the roof and boarded a cab to fly the ten miles to his home on the north side of the city.

As the cab descended toward the house minutes later, Harry looked down and saw Max's purple-and-pink flymobile parked in front of the garage. There were no lights showing in any of the windows of the house. Harry groaned to himself and decided he was in no mood for a fight. He told the driver to take the cab back up and head for the Holiday Inn a couple of miles back toward town.

"For Christ's sake, I've got important business scheduled for today," Harry fumed across the breakfast table in the kitchen. "I need a clear head. I can do without this kind of stupidity every time I have to take a trip someplace. Why don't you give growing up a try sometime?"

Lisa stared back at him sourly over her coffee. The skin below her eyes was showing signs of getting dark and slack, and her hair hadn't been touched since she got up. Women had no right bitching and whining when they let themselves turn into a mess like that, he told himself as he looked at her distastefully.

"What's the matter?" she demanded. "Can't wait to get back to your little pussycat in New York?" His expression darkened further, and she leered. "Oh, don't tell me that isn't what all this is about, Harry. It's Tuesday and you have to go back to New York already when you were there only last Friday. And you have to stay over again? What do you think—my head's full of rocks or something?"

"Take a look in a mirror and try listening to yourself, then tell me you'd be surprised if I was," he retorted. He glowered down at his eggs, decided he wasn't hungry, and tossed his fork down on the plate with a clatter. Indignation boiled up inside, and he threw out an arm to take in the whole of the house. "You get looked after okay. Isn't a guy supposed to expect anything back the other way? What do you want—body, soul, and checking account with no strings? If I fool around, it's because I've got enough reasons."

"All I wanted was a man," she threw back. "But I ended up with a small-time slob who thinks he's another Rockefeller." Her face twisted into a sarcastic smile. "Is your pussycat in New York another little innocent who fell for the same line about Malaysian rubber deals and Zambian copper stocks that I did? Mister Big Wheel again, huh? Bah! Everything about you makes me sick."

"At least that's one honest thing you've said," Harry grated. "Big money was all you ever did want. So, you've got it. Why is it a rough deal all of a sudden? I don't remember you complaining when you were peeling your clothes off for five hundred a week and probably making it up with extras after hours."

"I like money, sure," she spat. "Who doesn't? I don't like where it comes from or the 'friends' that come with it."

Something in Harry's chest nudged close to boiling point. "What about my friends?" he hissed in a voice that was suddenly icily brittle.

"Is that what you call them? They'd gamble away their own mothers' medical checks."

Harry's grip tightened on his coffee mug. "If that's how you feel, what was Max's flymo doing here at six in the morning?" he shot back. Lisa's eyes blazed furiously, and her mouth tightened into a thin line. He leveled a finger across the table at her. "I came back early on Friday but changed my mind about coming in. So don't you try any more of that crap on me, understand?" His eyes had narrowed, and his voice had taken on the mean note that said he had reached his limit.

Lisa slammed her mug down on the table, got up, and turned away toward the window. "Any attention is better than no attention," she snarled without turning her head. "At least he doesn't make me sound like dirt every day of the goddamn week."

"Why should he? He's making out okay."

"Why don't you just get out of here and on your way," she seethed hatefully.

Harry's knuckles whitened around the mug as he heard himself being ordered out of his own house, but he resisted the impulse to hurl it across the room. All he wanted to do was get out, but there was one more thing to be taken care of first and it needed a clear head. He looked down at the table and saw Lisa's pack lying half open with three cigarettes in it. He knew they would be gone within the hour. He picked the pack up and threw it back down on the table with a loud slapping sound. "Don't we have any of my brand in this goddamn house?" he raged. "Jesus, is that too much to ask as well?"

"There are some in the den," Lisa told him coldly without looking around.

He waited, but she made no attempt to move. "I never know where in hell you hide anything," he said, forcing a note of menace into his voice. He stayed put, and in seconds the tension rocketed to breaking point.

"Oh, for Christ's sake, I'll get 'em," Lisa exploded, and stormed out of the room.

Harry waited a few seconds to make sure that her footsteps were fading away, then reached in his pocket and drew out an unsealed envelope containing an opened pack of Lisa's brand with two missing, and the two that he had treated half an hour earlier in the way that Sandra had shown him wrapped separately in a piece of tissue. He unwrapped the treated cigarettes, switched them for two of the three in the pack on the table, put the two he had taken back in the envelope along with the tissue, and returned the evelope to his pocket.

The switch had taken only a few seconds but it had seemed like a slow-motion nightmare; in that short time his heart had started pounding and a sick, heavy feeling had formed in his throat and stomach. He clenched his fists and tried to force himself to calm down. There's nothing to it, he told himself. It's done now. Christ, why wouldn't his hands stop shaking?

He heard the door of the bathroom along the hall outside the kitchen close and lock, and breathed a silent prayer of thanks for the extra minute or two it gave him to pull himself together. He wiped his palms on his thighs, forced himself to take a series of slow, deep breaths, then got up and switched on the wall terminal in TV mode. A blonde with disgustingly perfect teeth was talking about a space colony or something somewhere. It didn't interest him, and he watched without hearing the words until the sound of flushing amplified suddenly by a door being opened jerked his attention away from the screen. Lisa came in and threw a pack down on the table.

"Only two?" Harry grumbled darkly as he fumbled one to his mouth and lit it. "What are we, destitute or something? Don't we have any full ones left?"

"Well, I can't find any," Lisa told him irritably. "Get some more when you go out. I'll put a carton on the grocery order when I send it off."

"Why do you always have to wait until we run out?" Harry snapped. "Didn't it ever occur to you to do something when they're getting low? Why don't you try thinking with your head for a change instead of giving it?"

The side of his jaw was still throbbing twenty minutes later as he looked down from a cab on his way to downtown Vegas. But by that time the air around him tasted fresh and free, and the feeling of everything he had just left being about to become a closed chapter in his life was exhilarating. When he next saw that house his troubles would all be over, and there would be only the formalities to attend to before he could begin the new life in London that was his by right because he had earned it. Sometimes making that decision to go for the jackpot and seeing it through was tough, but for the exclusive elite who had what it took, the reward was the moon. And Harry Stone had now proved that he was one of them. It was a good feeling.

Sandra lay back in the bed with the sheet covering her up to her waist and beads of perspiration still dotting the skin around her navel.

"I've been keeping a little surprise for you," Harry said. "What would you say to a bit extra on top of the insurance—like maybe a hundred grand, less the death taxes?"

"Sounds good," she cooed. "Tell me about it." Harry began sliding his hand down over her body toward the sheet. She caught his wrist and giggled. "I need to get my breath back, Alex. What's the extra?"

"Well, our friends back home in Surrey will be surprised to learn that my wife has been a stamp collector for years," he said. "I knew, naturally, but I was never that interested, and I don't know much about it. So I'll be as surprised as anybody when they tell me that she left some very valuable items among her collection. Maybe she never realized what they were worth either. Who knows?" He shrugged. "I guess we'll never find out."

Sandra emitted a delighted laugh. "Alex, you're too much! So what did you do—plant them somewhere? Were they to soak up some cash you had lying around that you didn't want anyone asking questions about?"

Harry brought a finger up to his face and tapped it meaningfully against the side of his nose. "Let's just say that even if they do lab test on the glue, they'll find it's genuine and has been there for years. It's the little details like that that amateurs trip up over."

"But not Alexander Moorfield, huh?" she said, turning her head and gazing at him admiringly.

Harry lay back and folded an elbow under his head. "How long will it take you to understand that I'm a real professional, baby? When I do things I do 'em right, and I go for the big stakes. That's what you have to do to survive in this world."

"And you sure know how to survive." She moved closer and rested her face on his chest.

"I guess so."

Sandra nuzzled against his neck and nibbled playfully at the lobe of his ear. "You really are a bastard, Alex," she teased softly. "And it's just what a bitch like me needs."

He thought to himself for a while and then asked casually, "What would you say if I told you I've been a *real* bastard?"

She moved her face back a short distance to peer at him curiously, but her eyes were still twinkling with laughter. "I wouldn't be a bit surprised," she told him. "Why? What have you been doing?"

Harry hesitated for a moment, wondering if perhaps he had misjudged the moment, but the half smile dancing on her lips was disarming. He sighed and grinned apologetically. "Honey, I guess you have to know this sooner or later—I'm not really me. I'm an Arabee."

Although he kept his voice relaxed and easy, inwardly he was prepared for her to be shocked, insulted, or indignant, to cry, sulk, throw a tantrum, or do any one of a dozen other things that would have made things difficult. But she didn't do any of them. Instead she stared at him in disbelief for a second or two, then smiled, and then threw back her head and laughed. "You *are* a bastard!" she exclaimed. "All this time and you never told me? Christ, I admire the sheer balls of it!"

"You don't mind?" he asked, not really believing that his luck could be holding out like this.

"You're still the same to me," she replied. "In fact

it's quite exciting. Meeting the real you will be like being seduced by a new lover all over again. I like the whole idea."

"Suppose I turn out to be fat, bald, and fifty," he said. "Wouldn't you care about that? You'd better say you would; otherwise I might start thinking you're only interested in the bread. I wouldn't want that much of a bitch. I've only just finished getting rid of that particular brand of problem."

"Of course not," she said. "So now go ahead and tell me it's just as well, because it was only a line anyway."

"No," Harry tossed out a hand carelessly. "It was straight, but I'm getting out of that business. I've got some personal enterprises that I want to develop."

"I knew it," Sandra said, sounding happier. "And I don't believe you are fat, bald, and fifty. It wouldn't go with your personality." She sat up and turned toward him with an intrigued look on her face. "What are you like?"

"Oh, a year or two older than this, maybe, but just as handsome. I've got a little bit of gray at the temples too. Does that sound okay?"

"Very distinguished," Sandra pronounced. She traced her fingers lightly across his chest. "And what about all these beautiful muscles? Are you as good as that too?"

"Better," he told her. "I used to do a lot of athletics. And I've got a much deeper tan than this." It was all too good to be true, and as the last shreds of apprehension flowed away, he found himself starting to laugh uncontrollably. His laughter triggered Sandra's, and soon they were both writhing helplessly with tears pouring down their cheeks.

"What about those dimples on the sides of your face?" she asked between sobs.

"I've got one on my chin, and it's just as cute." They burst into another paroxysm of weeping. "And don't worry about the rest," he managed between heaves of his chest that were beginning to ache. "It's best American stud."

After a while Harry began to calm down, but Sandra

was still clutching her stomach and laughing, if anything, more loudly than ever—almost insanely. He watched and grew puzzled, and as her laughter continued with no signs of abating, his puzzlement changed to concern. "Hey, Sandy, it's not *that* funny," he said. "Cool it, for heaven's sake. You'll get hysterical if you carry on like that."

Sandra wiped her face with the sheet and shook her head as she fought for breath. "It's okay, Alex. I'm not getting hysterical," she gasped. "It's just that you don't—you don't understand how funny this really is."

She wasn't making any sense. Harry frowned and shook his head. "What the hell are you talking about?"

"Alex—you see, it's—" She erupted into another spasm of sobbing laughter and bunched part of the sheet to her mouth in a futile attempt to stifle it. Harry's amusement turned to irritation as he began getting the feeling that he was being made a fool of somehow, and his mouth clamped tighter as he waited. "You see, Alex, it's funny because—because—" But she never finished the sentence. Her mouth froze half open, her eyes widened in sudden alarm, and she slumped weakly back against the pillows.

"Sandy, what is it?" Harry forgot his anger at once. "What's the matter? Are you sick?"

"I . . . don't know, Alex." Her voice was a dreamy whisper. "Sleepy . . . just hit me . . . Can't keep . . . my eyes . . . op—"

"Sandy? Sandy, say something!" Harry's voice was close to panic. But Sandra made no further sound. She lay with her eyes glazed and her mouth gaping as it had stopped in mid-syllable, with every trace of life and movement gone from her body. Harry stared at her horrified, and instinctively drew away and stood up. After a few seconds, a monotonous synthetic voice began speaking from somewhere in the region of her head.

"Please do not be alarmed. This is a malfunction of a remotely animated, nonhuman surrogate owned by remote-Activated Biovehicles (U.K.) *Limited. We re-*

gret any inconvenience. A recovery team is already on its way to you. If you need further assistance, please call 01-376-8877. Thank you . . . Please do not be alarmed. This is a malfunction of . . ."

But Harry didn't hear any more. He backed away in wide-eyed horror, unable to tear his eyes from the life-less figure draped across the bed. It wasn't the knowl-edge of what she was that was terrifying him; it was the *way* it had happened, and *when*.

Surely to God it was impossible. He gnawed at his knuckle and forced himself to calm down and think. There had to be some way of being sure. Then as his shoulder touched the closet door, he remembered the padded mailer.

He turned toward the closet, opened the door, and reached up to feel along the shelf. The mailer was still there. He took it down and read the address on the front: Sandra Parnell, 2754 Cunningham Court, Bays-water, London W.2., U.K. His hands started trembling when he saw that it had been stamped and mailed in the U.S.A. He turned the mailer over and read on the back:

> Sender: Mrs. Lisa Stone
>   Box 3683
>   Las Vegas
>   Nevada 89109

A strangled moan escaped his lips as the mailer dropped to the floor. But his anguish was not due to remorse over Lisa or the realization that Sandra didn't exist. It was due to pure terror.

For all of a sudden he knew why Sandra was always away, but always managed to be free when he himself was away from home, and he knew why she had needed to leave early on Friday, what Max's flymobile had been doing outside the house, and where the infusers had come from. But what was worse, he knew now why Lisa had stopped off in the bathroom on her way back from getting his cigarettes from the den, and why there were only two left when he *knew* there had been some full packs around the night before.

"You bitch!" he breathed as it all became clear in its gruesomeness. And then a senseless rage welled up at his own predicament and helplessness, and he hurled himself across the room and began pounding furiously at the unfeeling face and body. "*Bitch! Bitch! Bi—!*" he screamed. But the words died in a gurgle in his throat as a wave of tiredness and heaviness swept suddenly over him. His body collapsed in a limp heap on top of the other. After a few seconds, another voice began speaking to fill the room with a macabre canon of out-of-phase intonations.

"*. . . We regret any inconvenience. A recovery team is already on its way . . . Please do not be alarmed. This is a malfunction of a remotely . . .*"

Two lamps were flashing to accompany the emergency tone sounding from a monitor panel in the control room of the Las Vegas branch of Remote-Activated Biovehicles, Inc. "Hey, Al," the operator called over his shoulder to the day manager, who was coming out of his office to investigate. "I've never even seen one crash all the time I've been here. We've got two at the same time, and in adjacent cubicles. What odds do you think the guys in town would give against the chances of something like that?"   ☆

... All Ye Who Enter Here

Jack Williamson

The Great Red Spot: a riddle three centuries old. A giant continent battered by the insane seas of Jupiter? A floating island of frozen hydrogen? A monster hurricane, mighty enough to swallow many Earths? Or something stranger yet, beyond the normal human ken?

Nine years old, Derk Hawker saw it through his first homemade telescope. A bloodshot eye squinting back at him across half a billion miles, its mystery coldly mocking. He saw it again in the TV shots from the Pioneers and the Voyagers, from the Galileo probes and the Tsiolkovsky robot explorers.

"The riddle's too much for any machine," he told his father. "When I grow up, I'm going out to tackle it myself."

His father smiled, tolerant but troubled. Derk was an overachiever. The school counselors said he had lots of potential but unrealistic aims. Unless he learned to compromise, they were afraid his life could turn tragic.

He never learned to compromise. Always at the head of his classes, he earned scholarships and honors in a galaxy of sciences. At nineteen, he published his monograph on *The Riddle of the Great Red Spot* and begged NASA to send him out to solve it.

"Beyond our budget," he was told. "A light-year beyond—Congress doesn't love us."

"Suicide, anyhow," one space expert added. "Stupid suicide."

Jupiter, they warned him, was wrapped in clouds of

radiation hotter than the insides of a nuclear reactor. Men might survive a few weeks on the outer moons, but nothing alive could get past Io to reach the Red Spot.

"I'll find ways," he promised, "to solve the engineering problems—and to fund the expedition."

"The robot probes now cost a billion dollars a shot," the expert warned him. "And the Io torus has always been too hot for them in spite of all the shielding. If you think of going there—you're insane!"

"Maybe I am." He grinned. "If that's what it takes."

He never earned even half a billion, but at twenty-nine he did invent a better sun-power cell. With a fortune earned from that, and fame already dawning, he chartered JOVE—Jupiter Orbital Vehicular Expeditions. He paid for engineering research, hired PR people to campaign for international support, picked and trained his crew. By the year he was thirty-nine, they were taking off from White Sands to probe the Spot.

The media made tragic drama of it. Four chosen souls against the deepest mystery of the greatest planet. Hawker had searched for the finest human specimens who could be infected with his own insanity, all top achievers of his own stamp. The drives for support had won the world's admiration, coins from school kids everywhere, and grants from a dozen governments, but skeptics still called their spacecraft the Ships of Loons.

"Two years out." Lean and brown in his tight orange-colored spaceskins, Hawker waited to face the cameras after the others were aboard the shuttle. "Two years there to unlock the Spot. Or two more years, if it takes two more."

"Can you survive?" a newsman shouted. "So many years and so many dangers?"

"We'll unlock the Spot." With a hard grin the world remembered, he waved the dangers away. "Or we won't come back."

Two men and two women—he wanted no trouble with sex. Each picked for physical perfection, superlative achievement, total dedication. Hawker himself: astronomer, mathematician, cybernetic engineer. Peter Paul Petrescu: Olympic athlete once, trained astronaut and renowned cosmologist. Nicola Zarand: "Candy" Zarand as a college beauty queen on her way to advanced degrees in medical research, machine intelligence, and xenobiology. Rana Sindhi: dark-eyed charmer who had turned down a TV career to specialize in high-energy physics, magnetohydrodynamics, and astrochemistry.

Before takeoff, Rana and Petrescu decided to marry.

"No matter to me." Hawker squinted thoughtfully at Petrescu's male magnificence. "We'll be on our own." And he added, with a nod of speculative appreciation for her, "I'm in command."

Out in orbit, they transferred from the shuttle to the twin Explorers, one couple in each. At flight velocity, nuclear jets shut down, they linked the spacecraft by cable and set them spinning to simulate gravity.

Two years to Jupiter. A JOVE team at the Martian orbital station followed them with the new twenty-meter space telescope to monitor their broadcasts and transmit fresh observations of the planet and its swarming moons. The telescope troubled Petrescu.

"It could reveal everything," he grumbled. "While we're on the way."

"Don't sweat it, Pete." Hawker shrugged. "The Spot wouldn't give up its secrets quite that quick."

They stood watches in the unturning hub at the middle of the cable. Six hours on and eighteen off, beaming their brief reports to the Martian station and keeping their own instrumentation targeted on Jupiter and the Galilean satellites. Four immense moons, discovered by Galileo with his first telescope—all swinging through that plasma cloud, each unlike the others and itself a separate enigma. Callisto, Ganymede, Europa, Io, all turning the same dead faces forever toward Jupiter. The outer three, cores of rock wrapped in primal ice. Io, the inmost and the deadliest, spewing sodium and sulfur into that killer cloud. All of them convenient stepping-stones, as Hawker saw them, down to the planet and its enigmatic Spot.

It glared blankly back, sweeping them every ten hours as Jupiter spun. Swelling slowly, day by day, week by week, a vast and everlasting vortex, it gave up no secrets. Hawker hated it, or thought he did.

"Watch yourself, Derk," Rana warned him once. "You're too obsessed."

"Aren't we all?"

"The rest of us came out to get the facts and take them back." She paused to study him with a somber intentness and slowly shook her head. "But you're investing too much ego. I'm afraid the Spot will never let you go."

Five months out, Petrescu was waiting in the hub for Rana to relieve him. It was Hawker instead who came up the cable, a lean little elf in the tight orange spaceskins. Floating easily in free-fall, he read the records, checked the instruments, and swam over to Petrescu.

"By the way—" He nodded amiably at the cable he had climbed. "We're exchanging."

"What?"

"Nikki's waiting for you. She'll take the following watch, while I'm with Rana—"

Breathless, speechless, Petrescu tried to fight. He was fit as ever, a hard bronze giant, but he forgot the lack of gravity. His fury flung him sprawling off the deck into midair.

"Cool it, Pete." Hawker tossed him a holdrope. "We're scientists, after all. Not jungle animals. The women are willing, and you know I'm in charge."

Petrescu caught the rope and tried to stifle his anger. The mission had to come first. He had accepted Hawker's law. Trembling with bottled-up emotion, he slid down the cable to Nikki and found her in the hydroponic bay.

Stripped to shorts and halter, she had been tending the plants. The bay was hot and odorous. With water recycled and precious, their baths were rationed. Shining with sweat, pale hair bound in a bright-red kerchief, she smelled like her healthy self.

Aglow with a silent expectation, she helped peel off his spaceskins. She caught a lingering reek of Petrescu's rank maleness among the mingled scents and almost turned away before he saw her shucking off the halter and opening her arms.

Suddenly, surprised, he found that he too was willing.

Hoping to defuse tensions, Hawker called them all back together at the end of the watch, to air his own theory of the Spot. It was colder in the hub. Floating on the ropes, they loosened the spaceskins but kept them on. The fans stirred a stale reek of mixed chemicals and old sweat.

"A notion I've kept to myself," Hawker began. "Because it may seem a little far out. In print, it might have cut off half our grants. Some of you will doubt it now."

Quizzically, he squinted at Petrescu. "Of course I know the Spot's a storm. A cyclonic storm that never dies. First observed three hundred years ago. Tens of thousands of kilometers across. Winds in it blowing hundreds of kilometers an hour. It shrinks and grows again, drifts back and forth, keeps going forever.

"Driven by—what?"

Petrescu was hauling at the holdrope to plunge his big body forward and back again, scowling with an impatience he wasn't trying to contain.

"Heat, of course." Hawker shrugged at him. "That's what drives our tropical storms on Earth. Latent heat in water vapor sucked off sun-warmed oceans. But that process can't explain the Spot. Jupiter's a gas planet. It has no oceans."

"Derk, dear, it does have heat," Nicola spoke gently but quickly, as if to forestall some slash from Petrescu, "from gravitational contraction. The planet radiates twice the energy it gets from the Sun."

"We've computed that." He gave her a grateful grin. "What we can't compute is any mechanism to concentrate it under the Spot. There has to be something else."

"A solar component?" Rana's accurate English had a
faint but fascinating Hindi accent. Though her quiet
tone seemed almost too respectful now, her lowered
eyes flashed him a fleeting invitation. "The Spot is
dark enough to absorb solar heat the rest of the planet
would reflect."

"Thank you, Dr. Sindhi." He took care to seem formal. "That too has been computed. Jupiter is a long
way out from the Sun. The effect is there, but not sufficient."

"Sir"—Petrescu seldom called him sir—"what else
could be sufficient?"

"Eliminating every other factor—" Careful, still, he
looked away from Rana's secret glee. "I think the heat
is due to biological activity."

"Life in the Spot?" Petrescu snorted. "You and Carl
Sagan!"

He looked at the women. Rana was floating slowly
toward him on her holdrope, her dark half smile enigmatic, relaxed as if nothing mattered more than the moment when he would slide down the cable to her.

"You stun me, dear." Nicola's fond tone was halfway
teasing. "What sort of biology could create such immense effects?"

"I hope to find out—"

"If you're a fool, we'll all find that out!"

"Please, Pete!" Nicola shook a pink finger at him.
"If we knew what makes the Spot, we wouldn't be
here."

Petrescu drew a noisy breath and gripped the hold
rope harder, his bronze fists pale with pressure.

"If we're scientists, let's do science." He was too
loud. "Frankly, sir, I prefer a notion of my own. That
the Spot has a tidal drive."

"An old idea." Hawker shrugged it off. "Not sufficient."

"Never really tested." Petrescu hauled at the rope,
darting at him. "Our own Moon creates effects enough
on Earth. Here we have four major moons, one larger
than the planet Mercury. If you'll compute the tidal dif-

ferentials on the Jovian atmosphere, you'll find a shear effect between the zonal jets—"

"I did compute—"

"Derk! Pete!" Nicola reached for the ropes to draw them apart. "Let's remember why we came. The only question now is where do we begin."

"On Callisto," Hawker said. "The radiation there ought to be endurable. If the shields hold up, we can move on to Ganymede and I think Europa. Maybe even to Io—"

"Io?" In prim contempt, Petrescu called it *Ee*-o. "With luck we'd live two minutes there."

"If you wish you'd stayed on Earth—" Hawker caught himself. "We'll take the risks we must."

Drifting on the ropes, they all looked at him. Petrescu bleakly scowling, Nicola reaching again to restrain him, Rana's dark eyes wide with dread, that secret smile erased. A radiation counter clicked. A fan whirred gently, stirring the odorous chill.

"We're all afraid," Nicola said. "But we'll do what we must."

Petrescu grunted.

"We knew the risks," she told him. "Before we made our bargain—"

"With an arrogant maniac?"

"With science, Pete."

"So we'll go on." His tone was bleakly sardonic. "So long as we are scientists."

Hawker followed Rana out of the hub and down their cable, and the coupled spacecraft whirled on toward Jupiter. The planet grew against black space ahead, swelling slowly through the weeks and the unending months, until at last it ballooned, too huge for their telescopes, yellow-belted and strangely pocked, suddenly overwhelming. The widening Spot swept them every ten hours, a huger, redder, stranger eye.

"I can't help wishing, Derk," Rana whispered once, shivering in his arms. "Wishing you hadn't said you thought it was alive. I can't imagine how it could be, yet the notion haunts me. I get dreadful dreams about it."

They spun on into the planet's vast magnetic field, down into the clouds of trapped particles and always hotter radiation. The unshielded hub had to be dismantled. At the last meeting in it, Hawker told the others that he and Nikki were coming back together. Though Rana seemed serene, Petrescu turned grim again, no better pleased to have her back than he had been to lose her.

"Can't help it, sir," he muttered at Hawker, less than half apologetic. "Guess I am a jungle animal."

"No matter now." Hawker shrugged. "Gametime's over. We've got hard science to do."

They uncoupled the Explorers and restarted the reactors, first to power the supercooled coils in their own magnetic shields and then to brake for Callisto. In the cockpit of Explorer I, Hawker led them down across the equatorial basin, that vast bull's-eye where some ancient cataclysm had left its frozen print in ripple-ridges across two thousand kilometers of ice. They landed beyond it, inside a ten-kilometer crater.

Tumbling out in orange spaceskins, they all stopped to stare. A cragged black moonscape of age-frozen mud, splashed here and there with white, where impacting masses of cleaner ice had shattered perhaps a billion years ago. Jupiter was spinning in the inky sky, the Spot vast and glaring.

With heat from the nukes, they carved radiation shelters, condensing steam to refill the mass-tanks and replace lost oxygen. Such things accomplished, the search began. Deep inside the chilly refuge, they read telemetry, frowned over monitor screens, groped for truth beneath the dance of digits and the flicker of shifting images.

Rana was all scientist now, concentrating on the magnetosphere and the clouds of death it held around them, on the killer ions that sputtered and erupted from volcanic Io, on the cosmic dynamo that drove the Jovian auroras. "A million facts," she whispered once to Hawker, lying unresponsive in his arms when they shared the same ice-carved cave. "No answers yet." Consumed by Jupiter, she had nothing left for love.

Petrescu had no more. Wanting neither woman now, he slept and ate in his own frozen den, spending all his days on the swift-moving moons and the rivers of cloud that raced across the planet's blazing face, toiling to support his notion that tidal drag could explain the Spot. Morosely silent, he claimed no progress.

Nicola played no chess. Wrapped up in their greater game, glowing with a vital cheer that sometimes irked the others, she probed for gravitational or magnetic anomalies beneath the surface clouds, for thermal effects of the Io flux, for hot spots from deep convection. Failure never dismayed her, though Hawker himself was often depressed.

"Our time's running out," he admitted once. "You know, Nik—I guess it's pure imagination, but I can't help a sense of malice in the Spot. The way it creeps and leers—"

"You're letting it haunt you." She laughed at him. "Come along to bed."

Sex was yet another game, one she played with a dispassionate but total skill. Warm and wonderful in his cold sleeping bag, inventing new uses for the lighter lunar gravitation, she helped him keep hope alive, even after Rana's recurrent dreams had begun to haunt them all.

"Inexplicable dreams." She reported them reluctantly, her voice hushed and hesitant, the Hindi accent stronger. "Suggested, I suppose, by your own notion of biological activity in the Spot, but still—strange!"

They were sitting over coffee, rationed and precious, in the frost-glinting cave they used for a galley. Puzzled by her agitation, he waited for her to go on.

"Strange! Because they're all the same. I get a—a feeling of the Spot. Alive, perhaps, in its own way, but not like any life on Earth. It exists alone—I guess it somehow evolved alone—and it had never known another mind. Not till it felt us."

Hawker had to remind himself that this was just a dream.

"It's terribly—I guess *astounded* would be the word, though it has no words—astounded that other minds exist. Afraid, I suppose. Machines are utterly strange, because its world is all whirling gases, with nothing solid anywhere. It never even imagined metal.

"Most of all, it's perplexed by us. Because it's all one. It can't understand how we can be so—so separate. It can't understand how we could come from Earth alone. Or anything we do. Not even sex—or do you think I'm cracking up?"

She checked herself, staring uneasily at Hawker.

"I don't know what to think," she whispered. "We're all under such terrible tension. I thought at first it had to be hallucination. But it keeps coming back, and it seems so very real—"

"We are in trouble." Hawker nodded. "Getting nowhere, and picking up too much radiation. Time to move."

He called the others in to announce that they were going on to Ganymede.

"Out of one hell?" Petrescu muttered. "Into a hotter one!"

"True enough," he said. "But we halve our distance out. Gain a better vantage point from which to study everything—the inner moons, the ring and the auroras, the zonal circulation, the Spot itself."

"If—" Rana shuddered—"if we must."

Her shivery voice dried up.

Ganymede, the hugest of the moons. Itself an enigma four billion years old: cratered highlands of dark and dirty ice, broken with queerly ridged and younger lowlands. They landed on another crater floor, a cragged ice-scape lying strange and dead beneath a huger, brighter-blazing Jupiter.

"If it's life you're looking for—" Petrescu called to Hawker as they struggled outside to string the long arrays of instruments. Voice harsh in the helmet radio, he turned to gesture at the desolate black horizon. "No motion here in the last billion years!"

Hawker didn't try to reply. Working fast in that airless yellow deadliness, they tested the telemetry and rigged the nukes to melt out a deeper radiation refuge. Probing for whatever drove the Spot, they scanned it with telescope and spectroscope, measured zonal velocities and computed shear effects, computed temperatures and densities, looking for convergence below it, upwelling within it, divergence above. All that for nothing, but Rana dreamed again, this time that she was down inside it.

"I thought it was trying—" The Hindi twang was strong in her haunted voice when she came to Hawker, down in their cold common room. "Trying to show us what we're looking for. Not that it made much sense."

Her eyes were wide and dark, full of troubled wonder.

"I thought it was—bubbling. Bubbles of hot hydrogen boiling up everywhere, like tiny golden balloons. Seething up through those hurricane winds. Each one finally bursting, with a flash of reddish light. The flashes—"

Her own perplexity checked her.

"They came in the queerest sort of unison, making slow waves of brightness that rippled through the Spot. It felt my puzzlement about them, and we were just as strange to it. It wanted us to come down closer, so we could understand each other. I thought it was shocked—and utterly baffled—when I said we couldn't, because we would die.

"Dying, you see, is something it had never even imagined. It has lived almost forever. Perhaps it was frightened, too, because that's the end of the dream." She shrugged uneasily. "That's it, Derk. I don't know what it means, if it means anything. I just don't know."

Hawker studied her across their cooling coffee, trying to appear more cheerful than he felt. Problems with the instrument array had taken her outside too many times. Though she had not reported any illness, he thought she looked pale and unwell.

"Try to relax," he advised her. "Get what rest you can. And make the best of Pete." Regretfully, he added, "I'm afraid we will have to go closer—"

"Derk!" Her coffee mug rattled on the tray. "I don't want to die!"

"We're trading our lives." Gently, he leaned to touch her trembling arm. "We must get all we're worth."

Petrescu flushed with defiance when he announced that they must move, but Nicola stepped quickly to his side.

"Derk, let's us—" Her voice and her smile were as lightly bright as if she had been suggesting a summer picnic. "Let the main base stay here while you and I make a dash down to Europa to set up a satellite station."

Petrescu muttered sourly that they were never to get back, and Rana clung to him for a desperate-seeming farewell kiss, but they took Explorer I down to Europa. A smaller, brighter, smoother moon, nearly craterless, crisscrossed with endless darker streaks that perhaps were fracture zones where ancient impacts had shattered its thinner mantle of ice.

They didn't stay to make a shelter. Exposing themselves only in brief dashes outside the shielded spacecraft, they strung out the cables, hooked up the telemetry, erected the antenna, and took off again for Ganymede.

Closer still to Jupiter, immersed in far vaster energies, the satellite station bombarded them with data for two hectic-seeming months and then abruptly failed, the old riddle of the Spot still unresolved.

"We'll have to try Io."

Astonished, Hawker stared at Rana. They were sitting over hoarded half cups of weak coffee in the frigid common room. She had lost more flesh. Even her form-hugging spaceskins had grown too large. Her dark-circled eyes seemed hollow and too bright.

"You're crazy—" Petrescu caught himself. "My dear, I'm afraid you aren't well."

"Our last chance." She looked at each of them, with a wan and wistful smile, and slowly shook her head. "I'll go."

"Kill yourself?" Petrescu rasped. "For nothing?"

"Perhaps for something. If we're looking for life, Io is more alive than any other moon. Hot with vulcanism. The whole surface new—changing even as we watch. We need to know more about it than we do."

"Stop her!" Petrescu swung to challenge Hawker. "You can't let her give her life—" His hoarse outburst died when he saw that Hawker would not move to stop her.

They refilled the mass-tanks of Explorer II, and she took it up alone, the shield coils pushed to twice their tested overload. Down on Io, she called back through Jovian thunder that drowned half her words. Though her full array of instruments was never deployed, she had been able to hook up the magnetometers and plasma sensors and program the craft's own telescope to follow the Spot as Jupiter spun.

"Down in hell!" Her far voice rose and fell on roaring breakers. "If hellfire takes brimstone. A world of fire and sulfur, yet it has a deadly splendor. I'm near the equator, high on the sulfur slopes outside a hundred-kilometer caldera. Lava colors mostly reds and yellows. High scarfs above me, jagged and darker. Radial flows below, red and brown and violet. Jupiter enormous in a dead-black sky. I can see—"

Static swept her voice away.

Hawker was on watch alone when she came back.

"Derk?" He thought she seemed elated, yet rushed and desperate. "News for you, dear! Real data now, on the energy cycle. Spectroscopic evidence of organic polymers and other complex molecules created all over the planet by high-energy effects. Lightning, the Io flux, ions out of the plasma. Something in the Spot breaks them down . . ."

A crashing cataract.

". . . your own theory. The breakdown reactions do warm the Spot enough to support convection. The products spread away to mix in the zonal winds and build up again."

"Products of life?" His own voice was shaking. "Is there biology—"

She was gone.

For two days of strain, all they could pick up was that roar of Jovian energy. Hawker and Nicola were sleeping, worn out from long watches, when he heard Petrescu shouting, "—if you love me!"

Hawker stumbled out to the command pit.

"You're too close to that volcano," Petrescu was rasping. "If ejecta falls on the coils—"

"You know I do." Faint at first, her voice swelled until it shattered from the speakers. "Maybe more than Derk. But I'm where I want to be . . ."

The sound wave had faded.

"Get her back," Hawker called. "Ask her—"

"Listen!" White with emotion, Petrescu gestured for silence. "Damn you!"

". . . can't come back . . ." That roaring sea tossed up broken words. ". . . melanoma . . . these past months . . . very fitting finish . . . please tell Derk . . . dreams that seem . . ."

When the static swelled again, it was only static. Hawker claimed the mike to beg for more about her dreams, but there was nothing more. At the telescope, Petrescu watched her location on the north slope of that erupting volcano. A few hours later, he saw a bright flash there. A louder blast crashed out of the speakers.

"Dead!" He glared at Hawker, glassy-eyed, his stubbled cheeks drawn and twitching. "That flash was her shield, exploding when the superconductors went. You—you've killed Rana!"

"Pete, I loved—loved her too." Hawker's own voice caught. "She volunteered, remember? Knowing she was dying—"

"Aren't we all?" He staggered at Hawker and stopped again, breathing hard. "You—you total bastard! You seduced her. Seduced and betrayed her. And sent her down to die in that blazing yellow hell." His fists knotted. "You murdered my wife!"

"Easy, Pete—"

"I'm through with you. I'm going home—"

"You'll be walking." Painfully, Hawker tried to grin. "We have only one spacecraft left. We're taking it on toward the Spot. Rana gave her life for what she learned about it. We can't waste her—"

"What?" Petrescu swayed as if from a blow. "You aren't—"

"We're going down below the Io torus. Skirting it and the radiation belt below. Perhaps we can get close enough to finish Rana's study of that exothermic chemistry—"

"Exothermic bull! I won't go—"

"Please remember we're scientists—"

"Jungle animals!" Petrescu grated. "Except for maybe Nikki." He nodded bleakly toward her ice-cave. "We'll leave the decision up to her."

She was hard to wake.

"A crazy dream!" Shivering in her spaceskins, gold hair loose around her sleep-swollen face, she blinked at them groggily. "We were diving into the Spot—the three of us. The crazy part was what we found."

Her brightened eyes clung to Hawker, as if in search of something sane.

"Little golden balloons, floating up out of the depths. Hydrogen bubbles, I thought. Each one bursting, when it got high enough, with a reddish flash. All somehow in tune, so the flashes made pulsing waves against the deeper darkness. The strangest thing—"

She shuddered and stopped.

"Please, Nik, what else?"

"Rana! She was somehow speaking to us. I don't know how, because she wasn't in the spacecraft. About those bubbles. A vehicle, she called them, for the mind of the Spot. Those waves of radiance were like the alpha waves in the human brain—"

"Wake up, Nik!" Petrescu cut her off. "No wonder

we dream—living a nightmare! The way Rana died—"
His face worked. "The way we all will, unless we get
out—"

"It seemed—seemed so real!"

"Listen, Nik!" His harsh voice fell. "If you'll just say
we're going home, we're two to one against this arrogant—"

"Hold it, Pete!" Trembling, Hawker caught her arm.
"Tell us the rest of the dream—if it was a dream."

"That was all." She rubbed her swollen eyes. "That
was when you woke me."

"Nik—"

"Sorry, Pete." She sat up straighter, tossing back her
tangled hair. "But we can't give up the game. Our move
now."

With more current in the coils than Petrescu wanted,
they lifted Explorer I out of the crater and went down
from Ganymede. Red lights flashed as they dived past
the Io torus, warning that their accumulated radiation
exposure was now enough to kill them all in time, if not
at once. They dived past Almathea, down into syn-
chronous orbit.

Jupiter's bright-belted enormity filled half the sky.
Plunging around it in time with its spin, they kept the
Spot fixed below. With something less than Rana's special skills, they labored to decipher its secret chemistry.
Staring hour after hour into its red-blazing maelstrom,
Hawker felt sometimes elated, sometimes cold with
awe, sometimes simply giddy. Its mystery eluded all
their instruments, but Nicola fell asleep at the monitor
console and dreamed again.

"It was calling to us—I don't know how." She
woke in breathless agitation. "I thought it had—" She
stopped to shiver. "Thought it had a Hindi accent. It
could feel us out here, but it wants to know us more. It
wants us to come down closer—"

"Not me!" Petrescu yelped. "Not yet!"

They had reached the point of no return. From any
lower orbit, they could never climb out again, not even
far enough to refill the mass-tanks on hazardous Cal-

listo. With nothing left above the torus to relay their signals to Mars, whatever they learned would die with them.

"Damn you both!" Hoarse and shaking, he saw that he had failed. "The Ship of Loons!" he rasped. "Going down!"

"You're a riddle to it, Pete." She shook her head at him, gently reproving. "It can't understand you—the hate and bitterness you feel. Or much about the rest of us, really." Her bewildered gaze came back to Hawker. "Rana's pain and her death. Our sorrow for her. Or even the fact that we will probably die before we ever reach it."

"No doubt of that!"

"Don't you see—" She frowned, groping for what to say. "It has no way to understand us. Though its existence has risen from those hydrogen bubbles, they themselves are hardly half alive. Each one is nothing. Rising, flashing, bursting, vanishing. If we were something like them, it could grasp us. But we aren't."

"So it must kill us?" Petrescu grated. "Just to see what we are?"

Down, down again, into unseeable storms of killing energy. Jupiter grew, wider, wider, a dark-streaked sea of golden fire, stretched from horizon to black horizon. The Spot spread out to swallow them. A vast shallow funnel of rust-red iron, wound with darker lines of spiral flow. The wake of it, that endless train of lesser yellow vortices, crawled away and lost itself beyond the mad slopes of red-streaked, wind-whipped cloud that reached out and up, many thousand kilometers, to the funnel's ragged rim.

Nicola took the cockpit.

"Fly into the rotation," Hawker told her. "Level out and keep us up."

He put Petrescu at the telescope.

"To look for what? Circus balloons?"

"Report everything. And quick. We can't last long."

When Nicola tried to level out, the Jovian gravity

caught them. Weight doubled, Hawker sagged into the monitor seat.

"You're right—for once," Petrescu gasped. "Can't last—"

"Just report. Anything."

"Blurred red fog," Petrescu gritted. "What else—"

"Pete! Derk! I see them now." Nicola was joyous. "The golden balloons!"

Hawker swayed to brace himself in the bulkhead door. Beyond it, she sat relaxed and erect at the controls, smiling as eagerly as if she hadn't felt that pitiless gravity. Her eyes were closed.

"It wants us, Derk. It's spreading bright ripples around a point ahead, to mark where we should come in."

"If it wants us—" Hawker heard his own crisp command with astonishment, as if it had come from somewhere beyond him. "Take us down!"

"Damn you bo—" Something changed Petrescu's fury. "Sir, I've got 'em in the scope. Those flashing red balloons. Look for yourself!"

He reeled aside. Hawker toiled to the telescope. Behind him, as he bent to the oculars, Petrescu strained to raise a fire extinguisher. The savage gravity helped him bring it down. Hawker fell to the deck, blood gushing from his shattered skull. Petrescu rolled his body to the bottom lock and cycled it through. Reeling with nausea in the reek of blood, he lurched back to the bulkhead door.

"The bastard—dead!" he yelled at Nicola. "Pull us up!"

She seemed not to hear. Deft hands on the manual override, she was working to trim the hard-driven craft. As if unaware of any danger, she wore a smile of ecstasy. Her eyes were closed.

"Nik! Wake up! Are you blind?"

Mad winds shrieked, louder than the screaming jets. Metal shuddered. The deck pitched under him. He clung to the bulkhead, croaking at her:

"Hawker's dead! Take us home—"

"Pete, dear, it's you who cannot see." Her tender voice seemed oddly clear above the bellowing. "Because Derk isn't dead. Transformed, rather—"

"Babble enough!" His red hand seized her shoulder. "Up!"

"Too late for that." Her exultant eyes came slowly open as she turned to look at him, but she seemed not to see the blood. "Mass-tanks dry."

The jets coughed and died. The dragging gravity eased a little as they dropped. The spacecraft nosed up and began to tumble. Killer winds slammed them. Torn metal screeched. Petrescu slipped in Hawker's blood, and his own head hit the bulkhead.

At the Martian station, the JOVE crew had lost contact when Explorer I dived below Almathea, but watchers at the space telescope observed an orange-red plume that whipped out of the planet a few days later, reaching almost to the orbit of that minor moon. As it recoiled into the Red Spot, signals came again.

The spacecraft was lifting out from Jupiter, its mission finished. Structural damage had been repaired; the mass-tanks were full again. Professor Peter Paul Petrescu and Dr. Nicola Zarand were safe aboard, bringing their findings home.

Aboard, Petrescu found himself sitting in the cockpit with Nicola. Though a faint ache still throbbed in the back of his head, he felt remarkably fit, and he thought the cool air around them smelled delightfully sweet and clean. The stiff brown stains drying on his hands and spaceskins puzzled him for an instant, before he recalled, with a dim bewilderment, that they were Hawker's blood.

"We've bigger news for Earth, but we'll have to break it gently." Nicola had been sending, but she pushed the video pickup aside and turned with an impish smile for him. "News about the powers of intelligence and the shapes it can take in our infinite universe. News about Derk's transformation—"

"Derk's dead—" The fact was strangely hard to recall. "I . . . I killed him, Nik."

"His body's gone." She nodded, happily unconcerned. "Like those bubbles that flashed and vanished. But his mind's alive. More than ever. Picked up by that undying being and now part of it."

"I thought—" Blankly, he stared at his brown hands. "Nik, I can't believe —"

"Neither could it." She shrugged. "Not till it knew Rana and Hawker. Because it had no common ground, nothing to help it see us as we are. Broken, lonely bits of mind, hating and loving, dying and killing. Hawker and Rana helped it see. They're all wiser now. Maybe we are too."

"I—I did kill him, Nik."

"I guess you tried, but they want us not to grieve. They hold no grudges. Believe me, Pete, they've told me that—speaking with Hawker's voice, and sometimes Rana's. They've rescued us and healed us, rebuilt the spacecraft, lifted us toward home."

Still bewildered, he was shivering.

She leaned to kiss him lightly.

"From Derk," she breathed. "With love."

A Gift of Space

Margaret C. Hewitt

"Do you realize what you'd be letting yourself in for? It's suicidal." The boy sitting across from me was painfully young and eager. I had just destroyed his lifetime ambitions but he hadn't noticed.

"Don't *you* realize, Dr. Kemp? I'm going to be the best shuttle jockey that ever went through flight training school. I've studied and read about it ever since I was a little kid. I got accepted at Saint-Exupéry's. The HULAS exam is just a formality." To him the logic was flawless. To me the results of his HULAS exam were undeniable and far from just a formality. I tapped the graphic printout with my forefinger, emphasizing the condemning pattern.

"You can be a pilot, David, no more. You cannot leave Earth. You cannot be an astronaut, cosmonaut, or shuttle jockey or undertake any other profession that would require you to be weightless for extended periods of time followed by a return either to a gravitational field larger than a pebble's or to extended acceleration."

The boy shook his head. "You don't understand, Dr. Kemp."

"It's you who doesn't understand." I shoved the HULAS graph across my desk at him. "You have a classic HULAS pattern indicating predisposition to Vasileyev's syndrome." I thought to appeal to his years of devoted reading. "You *do* know what Vasileyev's syndrome is?"

He shrugged. "Sure. Anybody who wants to go into space knows."

"Then you know it's impossible for me to sign the authorization to Saint-Exupéry's." I felt as if I'd won some ground.

"It isn't impossible," he said flatly.

I skidded my chair back a couple of inches and clamped my hands to its arms. "But, David!" I said. "It's not a pretty way to die. And you would die. There's no known cure." He made me feel like a child killer. I looked away from him, through the Venetian blinds to the parking lot below.

"Tell you what I'll do," I said as I watched a man climb into his car, back out, and drive off. "I'll enter a formal HULAS challenge. It'll take a month or so. I want you to make an appointment to see me, and I'd like to talk with your parents at the same time. Will you promise to quit fighting if the challenge confirms your predisposition?"

"I'll make the appointment," he said. I loosened my grip on the chair. A different car pulled into the empty parking space and a woman about my age climbed out. She locked the car and walked briskly through the hospital's main entrance.

The results of the HULAS challenge returned in four and a half weeks. I winced at the comments the three predisposition specialists had separately included with each of their hand-done graphs. One asked permission to use the case in a postmortem seminar. "Genuine cases of Vasileyev's syndrome are so rare," the note said. "This would provide a case with fresh interest." Another note asked forgiveness for the challenge specialist's initial uncharitable reaction to having been chosen again. "Unusual patterns like this make up for the tedium. This profile is esthetically pleasing in the clarity of the predisposition pattern." The third positively burbled over my future as a predisposition specialist if I continued uncovering similar cases.

Corcoran stuck his head in to find me staring at the

juncture of four of the mottled gray titles covering the floor of my office. He was the secretary I shared with Wally Chin, another new doctor at the hospital. He had a headful of tight natural curls and eyes that snapped with amusement when he passed on hospital gossip or told dirty jokes. His proudest possession was a copper-tipped shillelagh whose history changed with each telling.

"Hey, Hannah," he said loudly. "Wake up. I buzzed you three times. That kid with the challenge is here with his parents."

"I guess we'll need another chair," I said after he had been standing in the doorway pointedly for some time. "Though about the only place it would fit would be on my desk." Corcoran left without comment, soon to be replaced by David and his parents.

"Before I go into the results of David's formal challenge," I began, "I'd like to point out that David's birth records include a HULAS graph showing predisposition to Vasileyev's syndrome. Having pointed this out, I'd like to ask you, as David's parents, whether you knew this or not."

A long silence. My view of the parking lot was blocked by David's mother. She was fifteen years older than I and looked something like an elementary school teacher I'd once had, a person who had accepted that many things which were beyond her reach were not beyond the reach of her students. Stray hairs floated about the woman's face and a fingernail on one folded hand was chipped or bitten. She took my looking at her as a signal that I expected her to respond.

"Yes," she said.

"David is our only child," his father explained. He was a big, quiet man who would keep a lot inside himself. "He is the only child we could ever have. My wife and I decided that what David wanted and worked for, David would get." Just like that. The family did not have much money. I suspected that David knew nothing of any costs borne by his parents. His father would remain silent. His mother, undoubtedly his mother, gave David his idealism.

Reflexively, I glanced back toward the window, only to have my view still blocked. I frowned. "I'd like to talk to David alone," I muttered. His parents stood and left.

"The challenge confirmed your HULAS exam." I pointed at the stack of notes and graphs. "Don't fight it. Your parents shouldn't have encouraged you this far. The birth profiles are done to avoid just this sort of situation. The best I can do is authorize you for training as an earthbound pilot. If you come back in the morning you can pick up the completed forms from Corcoran." With my view now unobstructed, I watched the traffic in the parking lot.

"Dr. Kemp," David asked, "have you ever seen a night clear enough to make you think you can play jacks with the Moon and the stars?"

"David—"

"Have you ever found Venus at dawn and imagined that she winked at you?"

I found myself grabbing the arms of my chair again.

"Have you ever wanted to run a footrace with Mercury?" His voice held hope and conviction still, yes, but fear also now and disbelief and anger.

"Have you ever even left this one town to see what's beyond the city limits?"

"David, I can't sign that authorization."

He opened the door and walked out. My decision was according to law, and any ethical predisposition specialist would have agreed with it. But I felt like slime.

"Corcoran, have they gone?" I asked over the intercom.

"Yes, Hannah," he replied in a carefully neutral tone.

"I'm going home, then." I walked quickly through the anteroom into the corridor, away from the loading elevator, and clattered downstairs.

* * *

I sat in a camp chair on the balcony of my apartment.

A house would come ten years later, but I was only two years into my specialty then, with no practice of my own. I worked on birth profiles and admission authorizations of patients referred to me by the hospital. Since every baby was profiled at birth and every person required medical authorization to work, every hospital needed a staff of predisposition specialists. It was a common way of breaking into a highly specialized field.

The night was warm and hazy and the city shed too much light for me to see more than the Moon and the few brightest stars. But I propped my feet on the railing, sipped a small glass of brandy, and tried to see what David saw, or imagined he saw. His imagery was ludicrous. The Moon was no rubber ball and Mercury was a hunk of rock, not a mythic messenger with winged feet. Why was it so important to him?

I spent the night there, getting up only to refill my glass. I vainly hoped for some miracle of insight in the lightening east on a par with Venus actually winking at me. Instead the Sun rose from the ocean and burned afterimages in my eyes. I rose stiffly, showered, and walked to my office.

I could always tell when Corcoran arrived. Self-conscious giggles from nurses and clerks always preceded him. He was outrageous, but entirely lovable, even when he concocted implausible limericks about the preoccupations of prominent hospital personnel.

"Hannah, help me!" he called from his anteroom. "Nobody else can. I'm working on a new limerick. What rhymes with *folly*?"

I was not in a mood to help him with his rhyme scheme. I had just gone over the graphs for the nth time. They hadn't changed. My Christmas-cactus cutting sat in its pickle jar of water and asked sweetly if I had thought they might. I said of course not, and told it to shut up.

"Dolly?" Corcoran asked. "Brolly? Collie? Holly? Trolley?"

Involuntarily my brain supplied the next word in the sequence. "Wally?" A chuckle bubbled up. "Not *him*, Corcoran! He'll take it too seriously."

Corcoran sauntered into my office. "Why not?" he asked. "Wally needs loosening up." He frowned. "You look like you loosened yourself up all last night."

"Not enough," I said grudgingly, tapping the graph.

"That kid? The one with the challenge?"

"Yeah. That kid." My momentary mirth had vanished. "I brought all his forms in here and went over them again. I'm going to have to disqualify him."

Corcoran stood leaning on his shillelagh, serious for the first time I could remember. "That'll be tough on the kid," he said. "I know how he'll feel. I always wanted to be a diver, practically lived underwater. I could swim like a fish."

"Yeah?"

"Yeah, but I was disqualified. Turned out I can't live under pressure greater than sea level. I'd gradually squash or pop or something. They showed me my profile, but all it meant to me was I couldn't be a diver."

"But you still swim."

"Sure, but it's not the same. I feel bad about that kid. He's bigger into shuttle jockeying than I ever was into diving."

"Send him on in when he gets here, will you, Corcoran?" My own screening fifteen years ago, when I learned the legal bounds of what I could be and do, had not been pleasant.

"Sure, Hannah." His serious mood dissolved suddenly and his eyes flashed with amusement. "Remind me to tell you what rhymes with *folly*."

He sent David in an hour later. The boy had lost his unquestioned assurance that anything he wanted badly enough he would get. It showed in the disconcerting dimness in his eyes that hadn't been there the day before.

"What brings on the symptoms of Vasileyev's syndrome, David?" I asked.

"A person's return to a gravitational field after being weightless," he said as if a button had been pushed.

I nodded, scrawling at the bottom of one of the forms. "Mostly right. A person could also cause onset of symptoms if he allowed himself into a situation of extended acceleration, since the two cases are indistinguishable as far as muscle tissue is concerned." I clipped the forms together. "Thus, were this person never to return to a gravitational field or find himself under extended acceleration, the symptoms would never occur. Theoretically." I tossed the papers across my desk.

David looked at me sharply, the light back in his eyes. "I'll be the best goddamn pilot they ever saw," he said.

"Look totally dejected when you walk out of here, will you, or I'll have my license revoked."

Corcoran walked in as David left. He closed the door and stood, his hand on the knob.

"You signed his authorization, didn't you?"

"I have some research that wants doing. I'm going to the library."

"I'll have to file your copy of the form, Hannah. I'll find out that way if no other."

"Start a new file, Corcoran. I'm going to write a book. A history book."

"Should be a gothic romance," he muttered.

David kept his promise, and we kept in touch. I received letters encrypted with my private key once a year or so, filled with descriptions of elegant trajectories and beautifully worked out fuel-consumption plans. Words failed him when he tried to express how he felt watching earthrise on his first shuttle trip to the Moon. David was no poet. His letters only encouraged vague yearnings in me which dissipated in the intervals when I heard nothing from him.

*   *   *

Fifteen years after David became a real pilot, almost twenty from our first meeting, I was heading the hospital's HLA research group, more administrator and promoter than practicing physician. I had my house and enough was coming back from careful investments that I could live comfortably, if not lavishly, without my salary from the hospital.

Wally Chin, my senior by a few years and former suitemate, had long since left for the West Coast to head a research group on the applications of HLA to cancer therapy. Now a high mucky-muck in the A.P.S., he had retired from active practice three years ago and spent his time doing research, fishing, and chairing the ethics committee. He had armloads of honorary appointments scattered at the top medical centers and was known for popping in and out without warning. Since I carried some weight myself, we got along all right by not stepping into the other guy's research area. A healthy respect for each other's clout kept us from blatantly sniping at each other.

Corcoran stayed on as my private secretary, saying that we could blackmail each other too easily if he quit. He filed references and edited my "romance" and never asked when I was going to have it published.

David was a seasoned pilot in charge of a scientific mission hopscotching through the asteroid belt taking chunks for further study. After his group had been there a week, I had received a letter from him in which he tried to tell me how Jupiter looks through a telescope when you're that much closer. He failed utterly and I set the letter aside to consider a reply.

That evening I nestled down with an after-dinner brandy to watch the late news. The anchorman was young and grim as he faded in with a backdrop of black night and stars.

"Eight men and women are fighting for their lives somewhere beyond Mars," he intoned. "The *Forty-Niner*'s mission ran into disaster today when an explosive charge misfired, killing the mission's geologist and co-pilot and seriously damaging the ship. For a further report we switch to a news conference just underway in Houston Space Center."

The picture changed to a crowded conference room with someone at a podium who explained where the ship was and how long it would take help to get there. Then a snapshot of David flashed on, and he was identified as the mission commander. A radio transmission, crackly and full of static, reminding me of tower recordings of plane crashes, was replayed. David's voice was much deeper than I remembered: "Jumping Frog Supply Base, this is *Forty-Niner*, do you copy?"

Another voice, presumably from the depot on Mars, responded: "This is Jumping Frog, *Forty-Niner*, we copy. This is not a scheduled check-in. What's up? You guys run out of Baggies?"

David: "Negative, Jumping Frog. We've had a small mishap out here."

Jumping Frog, serious now: "Roger, *Forty-Niner*. State extent."

David: "We have an explosive charge misfire on us."

Jumping Frog: "Were there any injuries?"

David: "Affirmative. Lara was out on a rock with Apummi. Both of them and the rock were blown to flinders."

David had listed the mission crew members in his letter. Lara was the co-pilot and Apummi, the geologist. Lara had been a close friend.

The operator at Jumping Frog said without hesitation: "That's two casualties, *Forty-Niner*. Any other injuries?"

David: "Cuts and bruises. But the hunks of rock bouncing off the ship didn't improve its design any."

Jumping Frog: "The ship's damaged?"

David: "Two of our solar cell arrays were smashed—one was knocked off completely. It was sheer luck our directional antenna wasn't ripped off, too. Half of our propellant was expended through several leaks in the primary tank system. As a result of the bouncing around, we are no longer at our previously reported position."

Jumping Frog: "Dandy. Have you got any idea where you are?"

David: "Near as I can tell, we're spiraling gradually in toward the Sun. Should fall into it about five years from now at this rate."

The picture cut back to the conference room, where it was explained that some fuel was left in a secondary tank system. The problem was keeping the mission crew alive until help got there. They had only half the needed electrical power, and without proper spin one side of the ship baked while the other radiated heat precipitously.

I forgot where I was and swallowed the glassful of brandy.

During the ensuing week I followed each newscast and read every news article. I tried to find Mars at night, but had no idea where to look or even if the planet could be seen. The distance between little blips on navigational charts slowly closed. Radio transmissions were replayed and explanations given of precious fuel expended according to painstakingly worked out equations.

The rescue ship rendezvoused with the macerated hulk of the *Forty-Niner* in time, but barely. The suspense, heightened by weaker and weaker transmissions from the crew, was too much for David's father. He died suddenly of a stroke the day before the rescue ship docked with the *Forty-Niner*. I attended the funeral with David's mother. Being the highly visible commander of a nearly catastrophic mission and the victim of personal tragedy as well, David became a public hero by acclamation of the mission crew, the rescue crew, and the newscast audience.

I sent him an encrypted letter telling him he was an idiot and that I was deliriously happy he was alive. He sent one back reminding me that he'd promised he'd be the best goddamn pilot that ever came down the pike and by tooky he'd just proved it. They were giving him a freighter to ride back on—no figuring of anything, all it would do was fall sunward. He made a crack about already having done that, and the letter ended. It would take him almost a year to enter Earth orbit.

Leaves turned color. The air turned crisp, then cold, and the leaves fell with the rain or flew with the wind. Letters from David were a little more frequent, complaining of the boredom of mere passengerdom after the notoriety of near disaster. I wrote back detailing the awards they wanted to pin on him, though he received newscasts just a little later than I.

In late winter I was at home bleeding over a chapter in my book when the phone rang.

"Hello," I said, trying not to lose the thread of my argument.

"Hello, Hannah? This is Wally."

"Why, Wally, what a pleasant surprise!" I said. "What can I do you for?" It was my old suitemate.

"I happened to be in town and thought I'd drop by for a friendly chat." Being convinced that popping in and out like Caspar the Ghost was all very innocuous and spontaneous was an affectation of his. Nobody believed the front, but Wally liked to think they did.

"Sure, Wally. You know the address. Why don't you stop by for a brandy after dinner?"

"Wonderful, Hannah. See you tonight." He hung up. Wonderful, wonderful. I went back to bleeding over that chapter.

All five feet five of Wally showed up on my doorstep a little before nine-thirty. He looked like the type of elderly Oriental who would pass out fortune cookies with beneficent fortunes. His face was graphed by fine lines along which it dissolved when he smiled. His eyes never smiled. He was dressed informally in trousers and turtleneck under his greatcoat, which I took to mean that this was going to be off the record. I poured us each a brandy and curled up in my wing chair. Wally relaxed in the Boston rocker on the other side of the fireplace, rocking gently. Cedar logs crackled on the fire, filling the room with an odor like burning hope.

"What's up, Wally?" I asked. "Want your profile re-done by hand?"

Wally sipped the brandy and let it roll around on his tongue. "No, not mine," he said. "Good brandy, Hannah. It was always your soft spot."

"Whose then?" I pulled an afghan upon my lap. Wally was playing his fish, namely me, and wasn't going to be hurried. I was willing to be played for a while.

"Let me tell you a story, Hannah," he said after another appreciative sip and a quick smile. "Once upon a time last fall there was a bright, hard-working and methodical graduate student collecting data for his thesis. He became interested in what became of people who challenged their HULAS exam. He thought of that point in their lives as a cusp in disaster theory—that it would make them or break them but in any case they wouldn't continue on as before. Being methodical he wanted every case, and started with records dating back almost fifty years."

Wally studied the flames through his brandy.

"Of course, given the privacy laws in force, he couldn't find out the names of any of the people. But he could learn why they had challenged, the results of the hand-done profiles, and where the people went afterward. The cases most interesting to him personally were the ones in which the challenges confirmed the previous HULAS profile. It took this methodical graduate student a long time to cover all these unsuccessful challenges. After six months he had covered thirty years, and his thesis was proving to be more interesting—and more work—than he had realized. But graduate students always underestimate."

Wally shook his head. I was beginning to fight the hook, though I hoped not visibly.

"Then, in twenty-year-old records this assiduous student found an anomaly. A patient had challenged his HULAS exam that disqualified him from admittance to

Saint-Exupéry's because of a predisposition to Vasileyev's syndrome. That wasn't extraordinary, though Vasileyev's syndrome is itself rare. Three hand-done profiles had confirmed the original profile and his disqualification. This wasn't anomalous either. What was astonishing was that this patient was given a medical authorization stating his superlative qualifications for admittance to the school."

Wally stretched. I wanted to spit his hook up but was gagging on it instead. My empty brandy glass gave him another prop.

"Here, let me pour you some more, Hannah," he said solicitously. "You can imagine, I'm sure, the consternation of this graduate student, consternation which was compounded on his learning the name of the doctor who issued the medical authorization."

He filled my glass and returned to the rocker.

"An undeniably illegal act performed by a young specialist only a few years removed from internship—a young specialist who would mature into one of the most respected authorities in the field of HLA predisposition profiles! What could our graduate student do? He went to the chairman of his committee, another well respected authority, and presented his information. His chairman decided to make an informal investigation, to speak to his colleague." Wally fixed me with one eye. "Well, Hannah, it presents a pretty problem, doesn't it?"

I was all but gaffed and netted.

"Do you care to make any comment?" he asked.

I was dangling at the end of his line, inches from the water.

"No? Nothing at all?" He leaned forward in the rocker and clasped his hands. "You of all people know the seriousness of flouting the screening laws! Willfully exposing a patient to known risk is worse than illegal. What you've done is morally inexcusable. HULAS enables us to prevent uncounted tragedies. Everyone knows that. They've known it since HULAS was instituted fifty years ago. Don't you have anything to say?"

The fire crackled. Taking a deep lungful of cedar smoke, I swallowed the hook and said no.

Wally stood up and shrugged into his greatcoat. "I'm convening a formal inquiry then. You'll hear from the committee." He shut the door behind himself.

I should have known he wouldn't land me without a camera and an audience.

The ethics committee met informally the following week and decided they had enough evidence to convene formally. Wally wanted to do it up with bows and ribbons by tracking down the three HLA profile specialists who had done David's challenge. The date of the formal inquiry was set at two months from the original meeting.

That was supposed to afford me time to prepare my defense. To make sure I had plenty of time, Wally recommended temporary suspension of my license pending the final recommendation. The full committee concurred. Since I had no defense and nothing else to do, I spent my time at home hiding, sipping brandy, and reading ancient articles on the construction of HULAS. I finished my book.

I knew nothing of the publicity Wally had managed to generate. He loved playing to an audience. I was shocked at the mob of reporters waiting for me the day of the hearing.

"I've no comment," I said to the microphones shoved in my face. I stuck my hands in my pockets and walked resolutely toward the hospital complex where Wally had staged my professional demise. My retinue of reporters and cameramen trailed along behind the whole way.

The committee had commandeered the seminar room on the same floor as my office, an elegant touch on Wally's part. It made me wonder if he had somehow managed to get a copy of my own profile. That was so unlikely, given the privacy laws in effect, that I dismissed the idea. But if anyone could do it, Wally could—whether he would if he could was another question.

It was not the same office in which I'd talked to David, of course. I rated this one because I was now chief of the hospital's HULAS department and also the head of a research group that added large amounts of money from government grants and private endowments to the hospital's budget. The room was thickly carpeted and had a huge oak desk, a matching sofa and chairs, and a private medical terminal. A crown of thorns perched atop the terminal. Oak bookcases lined the inside walls. My Christmas cactus now spilled splendidly from a redwood planter, overwhelming a corner by the window. I had a private cache of brandy that I often shared with Corcoran. The window had a spectacular view of the harbor, where I could see a young family getting ready to go sailing. There was a knock on my door as the father raised the mainsail.

"They're waiting for you, Hannah." It was Corcoran.

"Yes, I suppose they are." I stuck my hands in my pockets and prepared to plow my way through reporters, but the corridor was empty. Wally was being attentive again. He would be attentive right up until I was permanently barred from practicing. Good old Wally, a real sportsman, always played by the rules. I wanted to spit in his eye.

All the reporters and cameramen were gathered in the seminar room to provide Wally with a historical account of his biggest catch to date. They were crammed in the back half, standing one on top of another, all but hanging from the ceiling and clinging to the walls. Their number was exaggerated by my captivation with and antipathy toward them. I felt as if I were watching spectators at a lynching.

The members of the committee had taken their seats at the big table at front. I had a small table of my own facing them, back to the cameras, to their left. A somewhat larger table to their right was apparently reserved for witnesses. Those worthies were sitting in the first row of seats in the audience, separated from the reporters by three rows of empty seats. There were only two, which seemed like at least one too few. They both looked as if they had swallowed something unpleasant.

Wally looked as if he'd swallowed a canary. He was seated at the center of the table, flanked by the other committee members. I knew some of them, knew of the others. They were uniformly grim.

The room quieted. Wally banged his little gavel unnecessarily and addressed the viewers on the other side of the cameras. "This committee formally convenes to investigate a charge of unethical conduct on the part of Dr. Hannah Kemp, a specialist in HLA predisposition profiling and a member of the Association of Predisposition Specialists."

He looked over at me. "Understand that I cannot show you any leniency or special treatment because you're an old friend."

I liked that. He'd been baiting me for twenty years, ever since I'd told him I thought Corcoran's limerick was funny and not grounds for dismissal. If I was a friend, then his enemies were all dead by now, stuffed and mounted trophies on his wall.

"Other would-be irregularities must be prevented. Your former patient must be tracked down for his own good."

More like for Wally's satisfaction. He felt I'd trespassed, sneaked into his territory and stolen a fish from his private stream. Now he was going to add me, and if possible David, to his private trophy collection, all legally and properly. With true sportsmanship and a taste for the thrill of the fight, buttressed by moral principles as foursquare as church on Sunday and as old as Hippocrates, he would satisfy his outraged ego with never a soul muttering against him. Who could? He was right, I was wrong. So he said.

"For the benefit of the press, I feel a short explanation of the technical aspects of this case is in order."

Disregarding the reporters, Wally addressed himself and his remarks to the audience behind the cameras.

"The roots of the present HULAS technology extend back almost a century and are grounded in two vastly differing sciences.

"On the one hand"—here Wally flipped his right hand palm upward—"computer science and its subspecialty of artificial intelligence developed sophisticated decision-making concepts capable of being applied by machines. Early examples of these programs included a digitalis therapy advisor and a chemical spectroscopy expert."

He was condensing my twenty years of research, making the argument for HULAS sound straightforward, with wellsprings of historical precedent. He was good at that. According to the old news articles and technical correspondences, HULAS had been surrounded by controversy, heated arguments, and even impassioned street demonstrations. Shreds and tatters of this dissatisfaction and anger still lingered, but were never acknowledged.

"On the other hand"—Wally flipped his left hand palm up—"medical science slowly began mapping the genetic structure of human leukocyte antigens. These blood cells are an active part of the human immunological system, so, with a complete mapping, doctors could predict the diseases to which a patient is genetically predisposed."

Corcoran had filed a drawerful of papers for me on the beginning of study into HLA. Wally did the early researchers an injustice by making the process of genetic mapping sound so easy.

Wally brought his hands together and grasped them firmly. "The medical discipline of predisposition profiling was wedded to the discipline of computer decision-making when it became obvious that matching genetic structures to predispositions was overly complicated for a single person, even a specialist. Born fifty years ago, HULAS was the child of this union. The program is capable of learning, modifying its own behavior, and being taught a new discovery directly. Since the institution of HULAS, it has become possible to prevent a person from being exposed to an environment that would trigger the disease or diseases to which he is predisposed. Preventive medicine is no longer on the same level as reading tea leaves."

What Wally failed to say right out was that even after fifty years the mapping and matching was incomplete. HULAS could make mistakes.

"Against this background of humanitarian medicine, Dr. Kemp allegedly allowed a patient to enter an occupation, an environment, which HULAS had indicated would be harmful. Dr. Kemp allegedly disregarded not only the advice of HULAS but that of three fellow predisposition specialists, willfully endangering a patient. The purpose of this hearing is to investigate these allegations."

Never had anyone violated a public trust so shockingly, so unforgivably, as I had. If I had not spent the last twenty years preparing for this, Wally would have convinced me, too.

"We will start with Stephen Reese. Will Mr. Reese please step up to the table to our right."

The younger of the two witnesses approached. He was in his mid-twenties and desperately wanted to be somewhere else.

"State your background for the committee, Mr. Reese, then tell us what led you to talk with me in the first place." Wally leaned back in his chair as if he knew exactly what Reese would say. Maybe he had rehearsed the kid.

"I'm a graduate student," Reese said, "working on a thesis under Dr. Chin dealing with the effects of HULAS challenges on the patient. I started with the records when HULAS was first instituted and worked my way forward in time. The earliest records are some fifty years old. In six months I covered the first thirty years. In records twenty years old, I found an anomalous case. I have a printout of the case with me." He timidly slid the sheets of paper forward.

"Will you give those to the recording secretary?" Wally waved at Corcoran to pick up the case listing.

"For anyone who is unclear about this: the papers are official HULAS records and therefore, as required by law, do not include the name of the patient." He turned his attention back to the graduate student. "Mr. Reese, explain why this case is anomalous."

Reese squirmed. "I'm not really qualified, sir."

Wally frowned fiercely. Apparently Reese had stepped away from the script. "Dr. Kemp," Wally said, pointing to the graduate student with the handle of his gavel, "do you object to Mr. Reese explaining why he thought the case anomalous?"

I shook my head. It didn't make any difference anyway, since the three predisposition specialists would each say the same thing.

"Mr. Reese, please explain to the committee why you thought the case anomalous."

Reese squirmed again. "The first unusual aspect of the case is the predisposition of the patient to Vasileyev's syndrome. The second unusual aspect is the challenge, which confirmed the predisposition. Confirmation of predisposition isn't unusual, it's what usually happens now. Nonconfirmation was more usual when HULAS was first instituted." He was bogging down, had lost his place in the script. I felt sorry for him. Having Wally as the chairman of your committee wasn't easy.

"Anyway, the predisposition was confirmed. The patient then asked for medical authorization to enter Saint-Exupéry's. A predisposition to Vasileyev's syndrome obviously disqualified him. However, the record showed that the doctor in charge of the patient's authorization signed it instead of disqualifying the patient." Reese stopped.

"Who was the doctor in charge?" Wally asked.

"According to the HULAS record of the case, the doctor in charge of authorization was Hannah Kemp." I had an itchy feeling about the cameras. I wanted to turn around and make a face at them.

"All right, Mr. Reese," Wally said, having implicated me, "Let's delve further into the anomalous nature of this case. Excepting the predisposition to Vasileyev's syndrome, was there any indication in the records that the patient should not be admitted to Saint-Exupéry's?"

"Dr. Chin, I really don't think——"

"If Dr. Kemp does not object," Wally said with emphasis, checking to see that I still did not, "then there are no grounds on which you should object. Answer the question."

"Yes, sir," Reese said. "In my judgment, as a medical student and not as a qualified doctor, the patient seemed eminently qualified otherwise."

Wally ignored his student's qualification of expertise. "How many instances of predisposition to Vasileyev's syndrome did you find during your analysis of the HU-LAS records file, Mr. Reese?"

"Two thousand, sir."

"And of those two thousand instances, how many challenged?"

"One, sir."

"The case in question?"

"The case that Dr. Kemp authorized."

"Very well," Wally said, "what percentage of cases challenged their HULAS exam?"

"It varied with time, Dr. Chin. At first, when HU-LAS was new, the public was skeptical. Presumably people didn't trust a computer to perform the leukocyte antigen screening properly, so they routinely challenged the findings. And of course HULAS had a lot to learn, so a lot of the challenges were nonconfirmed. Over years of screening, however, HULAS has improved its techniques by self-programming and has expanded its knowledge base considerably, until now it is unquestionably a major authority on human leukocyte antigens. Challenges nowadays are usually confirmed. In fact, a lot of people think the three hand-done charts required in a challenge are inaccurate, anachronistic, and not necessary."

"Could you give us a rough percentage for the number of challenges to the number of profiles for, say, the last five years?" Wally had primed Reese for this question.

"About five percent."

"And of those, how many were confirmed?"

"About ninety-five percent."

"Directing your attention to the period twenty years ago, contemporaneous with Dr. Kemp's anomalous case, we might ask what percentage challenged?"

"About nine percent."

"And how many of those were confirmed?"

"About eighty-nine percent."

"Of those confirmed, how many patients were given a medical authorization anyway?"

"Only one, sir. Dr. Kemp gave it."

"Thank you, Mr. Reese," Wally said. "Dr. Carmichael is next." Reese returned to his former seat in the audience. The other witness stepped up to the table.

"Let me preface Dr. Carmichael's testimony with an explanation of why the other two predisoposition specialists are not here," Wally said. "Dr. Gorham is deceased. Dr. Trudeau declined to testify. All right, Dr. Carmichael, please state your original involvement in this case."

Kevin Carmichael, whom I knew only slightly from seminars and conventions, very carefully kept his eyes riveted on Wally.

"Twenty or so years ago," he began, "a blood sample was forwarded to me in accordance with the standards of a formal HULAS challenge. The only identification on the sample was a HULAS challenge number and the name of the authorizing doctor, Hannah Kemp. I analyzed the sample according to the usual procedures, looking forward to finishing an unpleasant chore. Graphing HLA characteristics by hand is tedious, as you all know, and I disliked it every time my name was chosen from the list of available challenge specialists."

I remembered the note he had included. Carmichael agreed with the opinion voiced by Reese that hand-done challenge profiles were inaccurate and unneeded.

Would he have held that opinion if his own profile had not agreed with his ambitions?

"The blood sample forwarded to me by Dr. Kemp turned out to be much more interesting than the usual challenge, however. The pattern that gradually emerged indicated clearly that Dr. Kemp's patient was predisposed to Vasileyev's syndrome."

"There could have been no confusion over the blood sample?" Wally urged.

"No."

"There is no question that the sample you analyzed, whose graph was included in the HULAS records, is the sample from Hannah's patient?"

"I analyzed and graphed the sample forwarded to me from Dr. Kemp. There were no labeling mixups or similar foul-ups. The graph was as accurate as I could make it."

"Then, in your professional opinion, Hannah's patient was predisposed to Vasileyev's syndrome?"

"Definitely. No question."

"Dr. Carmichael, if you had been in Hannah's place, with the results from the HULAS exam and the three challenge profiles, what would you have done?"

"I would have disqualified the patient. Everyone is given or denied medical authorization before employment to prevent possible tragedy later. I saw no reason to grant authorization for this patient to become an unrestricted pilot, and every reason to deny the authorization."

"You see no reason now, however farfetched, that might ethically have allowed you to sign the patient's authorization?"

"Well, one." Carmichael seemed reluctant to admit the possibility.

"One? What one is that?"

"I might have signed a qualified authorization allowing the patient to train as an earthbound pilot."

Wally thought about that.

"Thank you, Dr. Carmichael." He wiggled the gavel between his thumb and forefinger. "Dr. Kemp will now have her chance to present a defense." The committee members shifted perceptibly in their chairs. They wanted me to give them an acceptable excuse to slap me on the wrist and close the hearing. Too bad I couldn't give them one.

"I have no defense," I stated calmly.

Wally smiled hesitantly. It was as if a walleye had willingly leaped on deck at the presentation of the bait.

"I assure you this is no time for practical jokes, Hannah," he said.

"I'm not joking, Dr. Chin," I said. "I have no defense."

"Perhaps there were mitigating circumstances . . ."

"No."

"Then perhaps it was your professional judgment that HULAS and the three challenge specialists had erred in some way . . ."

"No. I concurred with their findings. The patient in question was predisposed to Vasileyev's syndrome. The profile showed all the classic characteristics, as our colleague testified."

"You're saying you knowingly granted authorization illegally."

"Yes, I am and I did."

"Why?"

"Would you believe because I have never left the city limits?" I received Pyrrhic satisfaction in seeing Wally flabbergasted. He shook his head as if to clear it.

"That leaves you open to criminal charges if your decision endangered anyone, including the patient."

"Yes, I know."

"Will you state who the patient is, so that he can be located?"

"No. That would be an infringement of his right to privacy."

"It seems he forfeits his right for the public welfare. A pilot suffering from the early stages of Vasileyev's syndrome is a public menace. Will you state his name?"

"No."

"He must be found. He cannot be allowed to continue as a pilot. He must be put under observation immediately for his own good and for that of his potential passengers." Anger showed in the set of Wally's face.

"No," I repeated. The process was becoming monotonous.

"I appreciate your motherly protective feelings," he said, smiling, "but extend those instincts to those who might turn out to be unfortunate victims."

"No," I snapped. "My motherly instincts are not a topic open to public discussion."

"Is he still alive?"

"Maybe."

"Did he leave Earth? Is he an earthbound pilot?"

"Maybe."

"Are you in contact with him? Do you know where he is?"

"Maybe."

"Has he ever reported any symptoms to you indicative of Vasileyev's syndrome?"

"Anything's possible."

"Indeed. So your conduct would seem to indicate. Is he aware of his predisposition?"

"Maybe."

"Hannah, you're being deliberately evasive."

"Yes."

"Will you cooperate with this committee in locating the patient?"

"No."

"Very well." Wally slammed the gavel down. "This hearing is adjourned until the committee agrees on a recommendation." He glared at me. "Your suspension continues in effect."

Pandemonium broke out as reporters and cameramen climbed over one another and the witnesses to get to me first. My answer to all their questions was a uniform tightening of lips. I wanted to go home and get drunk.

I sat stolidly until they gave up, then walked back to

my office with Corcoran and stood watching the now-deserted marina.

"Most of the boats are out for the day," I said, "won't be back till evening. There's a freighter across the harbor—Greek, I think. Would a ship of that size roll and bob like a rowboat on a choppy lake? How would it feel to enter a foreign port, a place I have never seen before?" I peered down at my pendant watch. "It's time to leave, Corcoran. Start going through my files. We'll have to clean out the office. Make a pretty copy of the book, first."

He headed for his own office without having said a word since the hearing began.

I picked up the Christmas cactus, set it against one hip while opening the door, and eased into the corridor. A single reporter sat at the far end, writing in a notebook. I walked to the stairwell and was balancing the pot again when someone reached around me to open the door. It was the reporter.

"Thank you," I said.

"You're welcome, Dr. Kemp," he said. "Do you mind if I walk along with you?"

At least this one was polite. "Not if you don't ask questions," I said, supporting the pot with both hands and feeling for steps.

"I can't promise that," he said, one step above me, "but you don't have to answer any of them."

"That's true," I laughed. "I've had lots of practice not answering questions lately. Who or what do you work for?"

The man smiled. "I'm a free-lancer. I sometimes work as a stringer for UPI, but you're too big a story for them to leave you to a small-time writer. They sent their bureau chief."

"Wally has a flair for publicity," I said ruefully. We had reached the first floor. "What's your name? I'd hate to have to refer to you as 'hey, you.'"

"It's Robert Garvey. I go by Garv." We were at the main entrance. "Listen, I got a car. Can I drop you and your cactus somewhere?"

"No, no," I said, shifting the weight of the pot, "I don't live very far from here. Walking distance." We headed down the hospital's main drive.

"How come you're taking the cactus home?"

I cocked an eyebrow at him. "Nosy, aren't you?"

"It have mealybugs or something?" Garv asked.

"Or something," I answered. "Have you ever been out of this city?"

"Sure," Garv said. "Lots of times. What's that got to do with anything? That's what you said to Dr. Chin."

"Good memory. An asset to a writer. Does the moon look like a rubber ball?"

"Not so's I've noticed." Garv was plainly perplexed. "Dr. Kemp, what's all this about?"

"Misguided dedication."

Garv was the only reporter there the following day when I came in to take the crown of thorns home.

"They're all out covering Dr. Chin and the other committee members," Garv explained as we walked. "Everybody's waiting for the recommendation."

"Are they?" I said. A light breeze was blowing, enough to keep the new summer's heat from being oppressive. There would be a lot of sailboats on the river.

"That thing have mealybugs, too?" Garv asked. "Or maybe it needs repotting."

"This is a *Euphorbia splendens*. Remember that. It's also a crown of thorns. Remember that, too. See the little red flowers?"

"Sure, yeah. It's kind of pretty. You really go in for indoor gardening?"

"Yes," I said. "It fulfills my motherly instincts." I winked wickedly at him.

By the third day I was wondering what was taking Wally and the committee so long to recommend the permanent suspension of my license. I asked Garv.

"Dunno, Dr. Kemp. What's in your briefcase? Got something hid?"

"A Pulitzer Prize–winning essay."

"I'll write the lead on the story."

"Thanks. Aren't there any rumors from your fellow vampires?"

"That isn't very nice, Dr. Kemp."

"Sorry."

"The UPI bureau chief says Dr. Chin ain't talking."

Garv missed a day, but was back the day after. "Excerpts?" he echoed.

"That's right. Think you can get them printed?"

"What's wrong? You jumping the country and want everybody to know how come?"

"We've all jumped the country, Garv. Most of us are just blind to it."

"You'd be great as a Chinese philosopher, Dr. Kemp."

"Thanks."

"I can talk to the UPI guy. What's it about?"

"Here, you can read the first excerpt. Corcoran and I have been working on it for twenty years."

"Kind of like your memoirs, huh?"

"Kind of. Let me know what you think."

Garv helped me carry some of my books home the next day. He was enthusiastic about the piece I had given him to read.

"It's pretty good. Too much technical stuff. It'll have to be edited, but it's pretty good. You got good examples people can relate to," he said. "How many of these have you got?"

"A whole bunch at the very least. You think it'll rain today?"

"Maybe. Look, Dr. Kemp, I made the UPI bureau chief a proposition. I think I can make you a good deal."

"Yeah?" I looked at Garv from the corner of my eye. "Why?"

"Trade? An answer for an answer?"

"No deal. I'll find out eventually. Patience is one of my virtues."

"Yeah. Well, see, nothing's happening with Dr. Chin, and the guy at UPI really wants something solid. He's running out of stuff for indignant follow-up articles. He says that Dr. Chin is keeping something back."

"Wally has legions of friends wherever he goes," I said lightly. "If it doesn't rain I'll have to water the cactus."

It had been over a week now and still no signs of the committee making a recommendation. I was carrying the second excerpt home.

"The UPI bureau chief really likes your stuff," Garv commented.

"He better, for the price you hornswoggled him out of," I said, wondering if I should invite Garv in for a brandy.

"Yeah. It should appear as a feature article tomorrow morning."

"Want a drink?"

"We got great coverage on the article," Garv said the next day. "I got some foreign guy asking for overseas publication rights."

"Any news of Dr. Chin?"

"Yeah. He's going to call you. They're reopening the hearing."

I stopped. We were half a block from home. "How come?"

Garv shrugged.

Wally called me the following night, after Corcoran, Garv, and I had finished clearing out my office. We were having a brandy. He said that the committee would meet in the morning to hear another witness and that I was expected to attend. We toasted Wally appropriately.

Garv sat on a corner of my desk while I pointed out familiar boats in the marina below. My letter of resignation was centered on the desk blotter. Somebody knocked.

"Yes?"

Corcoran stuck his head in to say that they were waiting for me.

The room was set up as before. Garv sat in one of

the three empty rows of seats. Corcoran leaned against the wall. The new witness wasn't there. But Wally was, gavel in hand.

He banged it. "This hearing is reopened at the request of the witness to testify today, who was unable to attend the previous session." He waited for the silence to become pregnant, then turned to an orderly. "Let him in."

The orderly opened the door and pointed to the witness table, speaking to the person outside. In walked David.

How can I say how I felt watching him move slowly across the room? He was dead but still breathing, a sentence I could do nothing to commute. He was dead as he sank onto the chair, smiled and winked preposterously at me. He was dead as surely as if he had put a gun to his own head and pulled the trigger. And there was nothing, nothing, nothing I could do.

"State your name and occupation," instructed Wally.

"My name is David McGowen. I am a licensed pilot. My last command was the *Forty-Niner*. My last ship was the freighter *Calaveras*."

"What is your connection with the case, Captain McGowen?" Wally asked.

"I am the patient whom Dr. Kemp authorized to be admitted to Saint-Exupéry's."

I screamed silently that no, he wasn't there, he was safe, in space, surrounded by his stars. But he sat there looking tired, answering Wally's questions in a voice lower than it should have been for my memory of him, dying, dying.

"Were you aware of your predisposition to Vasileyev's syndrome?"

"Yes, I was."

"Did you know what Vasileyev's syndrome is?"

"Yes. It's a degenerative muscle disease, irreversible once triggered."

"Did you know the triggering mechanism?"

"Yes. Return to gravity or extended acceleration after having been weightless."

"Yet you still wanted to be a pilot?"

"Yes."

"And persuaded Dr. Kemp to sign your authorization?"

"I don't know why Dr. Kemp signed my authorization. I am deeply grateful that she did."

"During the twenty years since, you have never done anything to trigger the onset of the syndrome?"

"No. I had no desire to lose my ability as a pilot—nor to die, Dr. Chin."

"Do you agree that Dr. Kemp's action was illegal?"

"Yes."

"Do you agree that Dr. Kemp's action was unethical?"

"No."

"No?" Wally played with the word, baiting him. "Her decision has led directly to your being exposed to a lethal hazard, and might have led to others being so exposed. I would characterize that as unethical, Captain McGowen."

David took a deep breath and splayed his fingers on the table. "Dr. Kemp fully explained my condition to me. She explained the implications to me. She might then have played God and made the decision for me. She did not. She allowed me to make the decision. I traded a great deal to be a pilot. I traded my family, my home planet, any mission requiring extended acceleration. But I became a pilot and a good one. You may examine my records. I waive privacy. Neither I nor anyone else was in any danger until now."

"How do you explain the death of your father?"

"My father was predisposed to strokes. There would have been as much danger to him if I had remained earthbound. His death is irrelevant to this discussion."

"Knowing your condition and its implications, you are on Earth now."

"To help Dr. Kemp."

Wally conferred with the man on his right, then the woman on his left.

"Thank you, Captain McGowen. The committee has

decided to adjourn and withhold recommendation pending your physical examination." He banged his gavel.

"Garv," I yelled, "keep all those wolves here." I ran to David and pulled him to his feet.

"Why in God's name did you come?" I asked, dragging him into my office. Corcoran guarded the door like an angry sentry, his shillelagh held incongruously at the ready.

"Take it easy, Doc. You're used to the g forces. I haven't been here in over fifteen years, remember?" He lay full length on the sofa. "Pretty snazzy office compared to the one I saw last. Kind of empty, though."

"Yes, I remember," I said, typing at my medical terminal. "That was supposed to be forever. Don't *you* remember? How long have you been here?"

"In the vicinity? Or earthside? I've been on the ground for a week trying to get old monkeyface in there to reopen your hearing. Before that I was at the medical station in orbit rehabilitating myself, working up from no g's to one gradually. You know what? All those no-g exercises that are supposed to keep you in shape aren't worth much. I'm tired."

"How long, David?"

"You mean in the station? About a week. Then a shuttle down here. You don't know how frustrating it was watching him fry you and not being able to punch him one."

"Thanks for the outdated chivalry, but you could have telephoned, for Christ's sake. Old monkeyface is going to fry you, too." I typed in the last of the description of the emergency requiring a medical shuttle and entered my authorization key.

"Invalid authorization," it typed back.

"Damn, damn, damn! I'm suspended. I can't authorize a medical shuttle. Damn it, why did you do it?"

From his prone position he said, "I owed you, Doc."

"Perhaps I can help?"

It was Wally, standing in the doorway, backed by reporters and cameramen. Corcoran kept him from coming in.

"Yes, Dr. Chin," I said, mindful of the reporters and hating every word. "I was trying to authorize a medical shuttle for the captain and discovered that I cannot. Would you be so kind as to authorize it yourself?"

"Of course, Hannah," Wally said, his face dissolving into a smile. "To refuse would be unethical." I swear I could have killed that little SOB.

Corcoran relented and allowed him in. He entered his authorization code.

"The shuttle will be waiting at the airport," he said. "He will need an attending physician for the flight. I've elected to assume that position. Will you be accompanying us as a friend of the patient?"

That brought me up short. I hadn't ever had to face it squarely. It had always been an annoyance, but I'd always circumvented it. There was no way of getting around it now. And Wally's question, asked with all his practiced innocence, made me wonder again if he'd somehow managed to acquire a copy of my profile. No matter. Now. I swallowed, feeling my stomach churning already, and said yes.

He typed that in, too, and said he'd asked for a stretcher.

"Gee, thanks, Monkeyface," David said from the sofa. Wally's face fell out of its smile.

"You do realize, Captain," Wally asked as the stretcher arrived, "that your license will be rescinded just as Hannah's will?"

"And you're not God Almighty, either," David said, allowing Corcoran to help him onto the stretcher.

We rid outselves of the reporters at the elevator. They stampeded wildly for the stairs, which I pointed out to them. The elevator ride wasn't bad. I was surprised. We went out through the emergency room to the waiting ambulance.

I managed the ride to the airport in white-knuckled silence. Closing my eyes, I found, made it worse. Looking out the side was bad—everything whipped by too quickly. Looking out the rear was bad, too—everything seemed to be swallowed by a whirling vortex. Looking out the front was the easiest. I fixed my eyes on an indeterminate point ahead of us.

"Hey, Doc, you okay?" I must have gone glassy-eyed.

"Yes, David, I think so." Wally was watching me curiously. Maybe he *hadn't* seen my profile. "I'm fine," I said firmly, gripping the stretcher.

Switching to the medical shuttle was done quickly and smoothly, though with plenty of pictures. The stampeding herd had apparently called ahead for reinforcements. We put David in a neutral buoyancy tank, then strapped ourselves in. Or, rather, the flight attendant strapped me in.

"Haven't you flown before, Doctor?" she asked.

"No," I said curtly and closed my eyes. "How long is the flight?"

"About an hour."

And I'd be weightless. I tried thinking about Venus winking at me and wished I were at home drunk.

I must have fainted during take off. Probably from anxiety. All I remember is the flight attendant floating over me with a worried expression. Wally was nonplussed.

"Are you all right, Hannah?"

Damn his sportsmanship.

"I'll live," I said. Convincing performance. I must have been green in the face.

We matched orbit and spin with the medical station eons later. Wally was quite handy weightless. The sight of him pulling himself along with his hands, hooking holds with his feet and pushing off like a little spider monkey, stripped him of his credibility. It was too much for my addled head to take. I started giggling.

The flight attendant towed me at the end of the parade headed by David, up from the depths of the neutral buoyancy tank. A room in the hub of the station had been set aside for him. He asked that his gear be sent over from the storage area he had reserved a week earlier. Still giggling, I was deposited in a corner.

"Hey, Doc, let me in on the joke, huh?" I opened my eyes to find myself upside down. Or else David was. Wally was definitely walking up the wall.

"You were right. He *does* look like a monkey!"

Wally was not amused. "If you continue to giggle hysterically you will hyperventilate and make yourself dizzy."

That stopped the giggles cold.

"Thank you," Wally said. "According to the information entered by Hannah, you've been in gravity for two weeks. Is that correct, Captain?"

"Call me David. Any friend of Dr. Kemp's is a friend of mine."

"Is that correct?"

"Yeah."

"Prior to that you had been weightless . . . ?"

"Fifteen, sixteen years."

"Well, the few actual cases of Vasileyev's syndrome recorded indicate the longer weightless, the swifter the onset of symptoms. Do you have any trouble maneuvering now?"

"Nope."

"I'll leave the room monitored and attend to some administrative details." Wally turned to me. "You would do well to orient yourself, Hannah."

"He's right, Doc. Grab hold of the handle there and turn yourself over. There. Now tell yourself that the floor is where your feet are." It worked, like an optical illusion. But I had to concentrate or different interpretations flipped in and I was standing on a wall or ceiling instead.

"Can't you tie me down or something?" I asked. My stomach couldn't take much more.

"Sure," David said. He sat me in a chair and strapped me in with a Velcro seat belt, then took a seat cross-legged in midair in front of me.

"David," I said weakly, "point me at some gravity. Real or faked, I don't care, but do it quickly."

His eyebrows went up and he grinned. "Sick, huh?" My hands went to my stomach.

"If you don't . . ." I began. He swam over, unbelted me, and dragged me to the door.

"Just pull on the rings," he said, shoving me out. "You'll get heavier the farther you go. And check with the pharmacy. They've got pills you can take."

I pulled myself along frantically, grateful for the returning weight. I soon had to turn over, because I was headed down, toward the rim, and I much preferred going feet first. I kept going until I was as far as I could go and my weight felt normal. My stomach, still protesting, began to settle.

The floor I ended on looked like a regulation hospital corridor. I had no idea where I was except in relation to David's room, which was straight up.

I stopped a nurse.

"Could you tell me where the pharmacy is?"

"Half-Earth-normal level."

That told me very little until I saw the label next to the stairs: *1,000 EN*. I started climbing up, watching for *.5 EN* or *½ EN*.

Half-Earth-normal level was labeled *500 EN*, the leading decimal point being dropped. The pharmacy was a short walk and easily recognizable from the international sign language adorning its front. The pharmacist grinned when I sheepishly asked for something to keep my head and stomach from spinning when weightless.

"It'll take half an hour to do any good," she said. "You might like to wait in the lounge."

This proved to have a glass wall on the side overlooking the rest of the station, the living quarters and "outdoor" areas. The view, with structures and vegetation wrapped around the inside of the cylinder, was so vertiginous that I had to turn my back on it. More than ever, the glamour of space was not self-evident. With a head light from the medication, but a steady stomach, I returned to David's room.

"I have a confession to make," I told him while he

strapped me to the chair. "Would you *sit* while I confess? It's hard enough with me lightheaded. Your being lighter than air is too much."

"I'm not lighter than air," he said, but strapped himself to a similar chair. "What's your confession?"

"Hm?" My interpretation of the room had just flip-flopped and I was conceptually hanging from the ceiling. I brought the room around before answering.

"Do you remember twenty years ago, all your terrible metaphors, the Moon and stars this and Mercury that?"

David laughed. "Yeah. I still use terrible metaphors."

"Do you remember the last thing you asked me before you stormed out of my office? The one after Mercury?"

He screwed up his face, thinking, finally shaking his head.

"You asked me if I'd ever left the city limits. Remember now?"

"No," he said. "No, I really don't."

"You did."

"So?"

"Can you keep a secret?"

He burst out laughing again. "I think so," he said. "Try me."

"Okay." I lowered my voice conspiratorially. "This is the first time I've ever left the city."

"You're kidding." He looked as if I'd just proposed that the Sun was made of yellow candle wax. "How come?"

"This is why," I said, and patted my tummy and rubbed my head. "Disequilibrium. Vertigo. Predisposed to violent bouts of motion sickness. Disorientation. Fluid in my cochlea gets jounced."

"But they have pills for that."

"Right," I nodded agreement. "All the pills either knock me out or make me silly. Aren't I silly now? And their effectiveness wears off. Silly, silly Hannah. Earthbound Hannah, walks wherever she goes."

"Your profile says that?"

"Yep."

"That's why you looked so white in the ambulance," he said. "What did you do during the flight?"

"Passed out."

"Really?"

"Yeah. Was worth it just to see Wally's face."

"*Was* it?" Wally floated in the doorway. The little monkey might have knocked. "It's time for Captain McGowen to begin his physical. Why don't you go find your quarters, Hannah?"

I was dismissed.

My assigned sleeping quarters were on 1,000 EN outside the hospital complex, which meant I had to withstand that vertiginous view again. I squashed the feeling that everything above me ought to be falling down on top of me and thought of placing one foot in front of the other.

I made the walk from my sleeping quarters at the visitor's hostel to the hospital each day to be told that David was not yet allowed visitors. Then I had to walk back.

When I was finally allowed to see him I noticed the change right away. He fumbled strapping me to my chair, and his movements were jerky, no longer fluid.

"How do you like the view outside?" he asked.

"Don't ask me about it! It makes me dizzy. How are you doing?"

We talked about his first shuttle flights, between the Moon and the medical station when it was being built, his first earthrise, and what the back side of the Moon looked like. We talked until the nurse came in and chased me out.

"Do you know where Dr. Chin is?" I asked her once I'd followed her out. "I'd like to know the results of Captain McGowen's physical."

"Dr. Mbele's in charge of Captain McGowen now," she said. "Dr. Chin left on the earthside shuttle yesterday evening."

I spent the next morning tracking down Dr. Mbele

and securing permission to see David's medical records. The results of the tests clearly indicated muscle deterioration, fast enough to show a difference in six days' time.

That afternoon David told me about his childhood, how he'd worked to become a pilot, his studying, his hopes and dreams. He said that his parents had told him about his predisposition, but that it only made him work harder.

A telegram was waiting for me at the hostel that evening. The A.P.S. ethics committee had voted unanimously to revoke my license.

I intercepted a similar telegram for David from the I.A.A. before it got to him.

David was confined to the bed now, strapped down with Velcro strips. I was belting myself into the chair and doing a lousy job of it when he started laughing weakly.

"Hey, Doc, you ought to take lessons," he said. His speech was beginning to slur. "You still taking your pills?"

"No," I said, shaking my head. "I don't seem to need them."

"Challenge it, Doc," he said, trying to smile. "It's worth it."

"Is it?" I asked. Was it?

One day he told me about the mission he had co-piloted to Venus, how intricate the cloud patterns were and how large the Sun. Then there was the mission to Titan, still in progress, which he'd turned down in favor of the *Forty-Niner*. He explained how Jumping Frog Supply Base was named and where it was on Mars.

The nurse said I had to leave. I stalled, floating beside the bed, asking questions about the care Dr. Mbele had prescribed. I was afraid to leave—what would I come back to?

David was on life support in the morning. He couldn't quite control his eyes and they wandered independently. His speech was almost unintelligible but he insisted on talking about the *Forty-Niner* and her crew. All that day I listened to stories of Lara and Apummi. I think he might have married Lara if circumstances had been different. Apummi, the Inuktitut geologist, had studied the carbon dioxide formations of the Martian polar regions before signing on to the mission that must have been a geologist's dream.

"I'm sorry, David," I said.

"Don't be sorry. It was worth it. It was worth the trade. Don't ever feel sorry you signed my authorization, Doc."

"Hannah. My name is Hannah." I was holding myself to the chair as if by my own strength, squeezing, I could slow the deterioration.

"Hannah." He said it. I think he said it. It was the last word he would ever say. He went into cardiac arrest while I slept that night, and died.

I returned to my room at the visitor's hostel for the last time after making arrangements to return to Earth with David's body. All I could think of was that there would be no more letters at unpredictable intervals, encrypted with my private key. No more unsuccessful descriptions of wonders I would never see, no more overwhelming details of orbital paths or computer protocols.

A man was waiting for me outside my room. He had curly gray hair and snapping black eyes and leaned rather heavily on a copper-tipped shillelagh. I smiled, genuinely happy.

"Hello, Hannah," he said.

"Corcoran, you reprobate. What are you doing here? Blackmail your way up on a medical shuttle?" I showed him in to a chair.

Corcoran set the shillelagh across his knees. "Have you been keeping up with the news?"

"No," I confessed. "I've been hiding. I can't stand seeing myself. I look old and fat and tired." He smiled crookedly.

"If you're old, we're both old. You do look a little tired and we are both thicker than we were twenty years ago." He patted his tummy, which was flatter than his description implied. "The police have drafted charges against you."

"What charge?" I had drawn the drapes against the view and now wished I had somewhere to look.

"For now, criminal negligence contributing to the death of a patient." That was enough.

"Anything else?"

"I gave Garv the rest of the excerpts from your romance. They're really eating it up. And I've had some offers for hardbound editions with subtitles like 'A Historical Criticism of Human Leukocyte Screening Procedures.' Snappy, huh?"

"Yeah." I rose, restless, and pulled the drapes.

"I'm not finished," Corcoran said. "Congress has created an ad hoc committee to look into revising the HLA screening laws. You've caused quite a ruckus. I'd even go so far as to say you're notorious."

"You would," I said, but it made me feel better.

"There's a group of us agitating to have the charges against you dropped."

"Your loyalty is astounding. Group?"

"Yeah. A small one so far, but interplanetary in scope. There's yours truly, your faithful servant, and my family, Garv, and David's mother. She's taking his death kind of hard, but she supports you all the way."

"*She* would."

Corcoran laughed. "The interplanetary contingent includes the seven remaining crew members of the *Forty-Niner* and the entire population of Jumping Frog Supply Base."

"That's all very nice but also useless. What I did for David was illegal. I was wrong. I knew I was wrong when I did it."

"I knew it was illegal, too, but I never turned you in. Never told a soul."

Looking out at the warped perspective of the hospital station, my eyes were suddenly moist. "We were both wrong. The HULAS exams are necessary. Preventive medicine. It was irresponsible to allow David to expose himself to health risks known ahead of time."

"Hannah, David knew what he was doing."

"No, he didn't. He's just a kid. He was always a kid. He never grew up. He never admitted that there might be something he couldn't handle."

"He knew what he was doing, even when he came back to Earth," Corcoran said, emphasizing the meaning. "He knew he was going to lose and he didn't want to spend the next forty years being pitied. And Wally wouldn't reopen the hearing unless David testified personally."

"He could have stayed here. He could have called. No, he deliberately exposed himself for two weeks. If I'm going to have my career ruined, the least David could have done was stick around and help me get drunk."

I was contradicting myself, but I didn't care.

"You knew it would come to this when you signed his authorization," Corcoran said. "Now you're acting as if somebody played a dirty trick on you."

"I didn't think the goddamn idiot would kill himself."

Corcoran said nothing.

"I'm gonna kill Wally," I said finally.

"We had something less homicidal, more legislative, in mind."   ☆

The Cerebrated Jumping Frog of Calaveras III

Martha Dodson and Robert L. Forward

A sting of fatigue pierced the unreachable spot in his
right shoulder as Dr. Ernest Hill bent over one last report from the computer. It really didn't look very prom-
ising; just another carefully phrased, machine-cold sum-
mary of another native creature that hadn't changed
much since its beginning, that wasn't going to change
much, and that would have to be left unchanged. Like
all the rest of the specimens he had examined on this
fertile but dead-end planet, this one had strayed off the
pathway leading up the hill of life. Lured on by an un-
demanding Nature in the form of an almost unchanging
climate, the life forms on this planet had wandered onto
an ecological mesa. They were unable to develop any
further, and it wasn't possible to evolve back into simpler forms. Unless a statistically improbable multiple
mutation caused them to jump across the chasm back
onto the right pathway, they were fated to spend their
second, third, and fourth billion years as they had their
first, living and dying, layer upon layer, but never,
never changing.

Even on a challenging planet, Nature took a tire-
somely long time to evolve useful, complicated, and
interesting specimens, but Man preferred to Do It Now.
On a fresh, naive planet such as this one, it was very
satisfying to play God. Controlled genetics between
computer-chosen individuals led to the development of

a new dominant race for each new world—one indigenous to that world, capable, intelligent, productive, and unhampered by any history whatsoever. If carefully selected breeding stock was insufficient, then it was easy enough to induce a moderate amount of selective mutation.

Even if doing so proved impractical, Ernest Hill could use any two animals, independent of age, sex, order, genus, or even class. Starting with one cell from each, he would rip them down to the DNA in their genes, eliminating all the cellular bias against mixing; then carefully tease the stringy macromolecules with chemicals, warmth, and controlled pulses of coherent light, take them apart, cut out the pieces that he wanted, and recombine them into a new, vital storehouse of genetic information. It usually required years to get a living cell out of the process. That was the hard way, a way that was professionally interesting, but not one that a Ph.D. working for a Phi.Sci. wanted to get involved in, especially if he had a family.

The unripe state of this world, so unchanged from its creation that its seas still looked like Chaos and its shadows like Old Night, meant that the meddlers in the shiny dome had a hard time finding anything better to work with than a rather lovely jellyfish. There was no real hurry; Ernest Hill and Frank Young, the biomathematician, had their wives and families snugly housed right next door, and the warp-radio operator and all-around handyman, an aging bachelor, would be just as dour on the next world. Twenty-eight generations had distilled a persimmon-like acidity in Thor Leip untouched by the frost of his native Iceland.

No one was breathing down their necks for results, but it was humiliating to the good doctor to examine captive after captive only to find nothing. He would laboriously analyze their genetic characteristics, argue with Frank over the importance of each gene—or lack of one—in the hypothetical and statistically fuzzy future social structure of a creature holding those genes. He would then carefully submit all the details to the indifferent machine, only to have them calmly rejected, every one, as "Unfit for Expansion at This Time."

The doctor was struggling with a most unscholarly resentment of the shiny computer's high-handed dismissal of all the offerings he had laid on its doorstep. His carefully cultivated patience was not bearing up too well, either, under the rather sarcastic curiosity of Thor. "How is the ol' Darwin doing?" and "Just like Kansas City—this place has gone about as fur as it can go" were remarks not calculated to encourage. Thor really had far too much time on his hands—only a little maintenance and an occasional laconic report to the base required his attention—and he had whiled a good bit of his time away, acquiring an amateur's knowledge of the jobs of the other two men.

"I think I'll quit for now," Dr. Hill sighed, straightening up and exuding both relief and discouragement, his fingers jabbing futilely at the unreachable sting on his back. He thought gratefully of Ann, who could soothe away the tension in two minutes. He left the room as it was. There was never any need to put anything away when he would be the only person using the equipment next.

Going through the door, he shed ten years, several pounds, his depression, and his coat. He advanced on all fours toward his reading chair. There, his daughter waited. The excitement of Daddy's arrival made her bounce like a yo-yo, sparking her face and boosting the volume of her greeting to an alarming degree. As soon as he was within navigable distance, she fearlessly let go the support, and, bare-masted, tacked breathlessly to and fro until she made the safe harbor of his arms.

Janet was one year old today and did not care a bit. Her parents were jubilant, though, and the rest of their small party gathered at dinner to help celebrate. Frank had merrily suggested that his beloved computer ought to be in on the fun and was a little surprised at the vehemence with which Dr. Hill denied it any place in the festivities. Frank's wife joined them, as did their son, briefly. He was ten, and Frank and Marge hoped to renew their acquaintance with the boy when he had emerged from the Video Thriller and Peanut Butter stage.

The radioman, with some slight instinct for the duties of a guest, unbent sufficiently to try to say something without a barb in it. He realized immediately, however, that the attention of his small audience went from slight to zero whenever the conversation was in danger of deviating from the subject of the small fry then present. So he relapsed into silence, consoling himself with mentally perfecting the details of a practical joke to be played on the proud father.

The children had adjusted to this new world as casually as children always do. Ernest and Ann had devoted a great deal of extremely serious thought to the problems of just how many diapers, toys, and larger and larger shoes, it would be necessary to pack before leaving home, so it was with a relief practically amounting to a letdown to see Janet developing so trauma-free and serene. Frank's son, young Stewart, gave his parents no worry other than that their tapes of thrillers might not hold out for the duration, but they found reassurance in the fact that re-watching the old ones produced the same glassy-eyed tranquility. The only problem Stewart had for weeks was this very same birthday party; he knew he would hate it, would be bored to death, uncomfortably dressed, and obliged to sit up straight—all a rather high price to pay for even such unquestionable delicacies as ice cream and cake.

While Janet was engaged in wrapping both sets of parents firmly around one sticky finger, Stewart and Thor conducted a masculine dialogue on the possibility of stocking the nearby pools with trout. Soon, however, the lowered tone of this conversation attracted the birthday child's attention, and the discovery that two of those present were not yet under her spell prompted her to begin an earnest attempt to bring them into line. Stewart was easy. The deposit of every movable object in the room into his lap, accompanied by two dozen calculated entrancing stares, and he was beaming pinkly. However, the radioman remained aloof; to him, Janet was as alien as anything on the planet.

Only after the object of everyone's attention was asleep, and the wives had begun scanning the latest news tapes, was Thor able to dip a tentative oar into the conversation and steer it toward the work in progress.

Ernest felt gloom settling on him again. "I thought I had a real prospect today—quadruped, circulatory system, almost an Earth-type reptile, but the computer turned it down. Too small a brainpan or some darn thing."

"Have you searched *all* around? Maybe on the other side of this continent?" The radioman put the question to him almost seriously—a few more months and he would be as anxious for an answer as they.

Ernest confessed there was much still unexplored. "Too much. There is a vast amount of life here—beings that differ from each other a lot or a little—but none of it, combined with any of the rest of it, will give us anything much different from the majority of it. All these red genes, so to speak, combined with all those white genes, will give us plenty of pink genes, but we need a black gene."

In the morning Ernest Hill set out on yet another hunting trip. To his cynical eyes, all the specimens in the laboratory seemed hardly worth bothering the computer with. On his trip, he found a few deviations from the current individuals he had been working with, but nothing startling until he had given up and was heading home. Regarding him gravely from the edge of a pool was something that looked so much like a frog that he nearly passed it by, noting only that it was a fine frog. Then he realized he had not seen a frog on this world before! Aside from being shiny blue-green and weighing nearly ten pounds, it was no prettier than an Earth frog, but Dr. Hill carried it as tenderly to the lab as if it were an enchanted prince.

Subjected to analysis, his find proved a trifle discouraging; the creature's characteristics were not as high above the norm as he could have wished. In his excitement at preparing the data for the computer—and his secret hopes for a break—he didn't notice that additional information had already been fed into the machine.

Carefully, he inserted his data into the memory and started the calculations. His spirits rose, in spite of his efforts at self-damping, while he watched the machine. If only this turned out to be a "possible," he promised himself, he would search patiently, even indefinitely, for the species to combine with it. With elation he heard the computer calling in buzzes and hums and whirs that had not sounded before, taking an unusually long time to complete the calculations. He scanned the output, his bewilderment growing.

The machine was not enthusiastic over his frog. In fact, it was quite cool toward his frog. It viewed his frog with much misgiving. But it conjectured that, united with the mate that had been suggested, it was quite possible that a big step upward would be made. The machine was quite enthusiastic about this mate, implying that this was the sort of "mate"-erial it should have had to work with all along, if progress was to be made.

Ernest Hill frowned. He had not suggested any mate. Someone had been tampering with the computer. A quick query to the computer retrieved the answer. The mate suggested for the frog was Janet!

Unfortunately, practical jokers are not excluded from the universal rule barring the taking of life, so with full knowledge of his probable fate Ernest Hill set out to find Thor Leip and destroy him in some lingering fashion. He did not even hesitate when he learned from Frank that Thor had taken the skimmer for an excursion to the mountains in the south. However, as the search for his prey lengthened, Dr. Hill found the enthusiasm of the computer for human genes first tolerable, then understandable—exactly what the radioman had expected, of course. Ernest's fury had spent itself to the extent that hunter and hunted finally faced off with a cool stare and returned home in silence.

"This frog almost has it made, Frank. It can grasp with its front paws and shows a tendency to keep them free from the ground. Its eyes are highly developed and it will eat practically anything. It has a brain that for size has no equal on this planet, but it's stupid—stupid as a damned frog!"

"Now look, Ernest, obviously, the main trouble is that there is no association going on in its brain. The nerve pulses come in from the sense organs and go right back out to the muscles without any interaction taking place. In our brains, we not only have full control over most of our reactions but can also use a part of the brain to create an imaginary stimulus to drive the rest of it. When a man rushes into a burning building to save a child, the artificial stimulus of the suffering child makes him ignore the very real pain of the flames on his skin and the smoke in his lungs. This ability to make imaginary models of the outside world allows us to formulate plans. But for this process to take place, there must be interaction among the neurons in the brain. I think the problem is that this frog has plenty of brain cells but he doesn't make use of them. I bet they don't have any branching ratio to speak of."

"No! That's not it," said Ernest. "It's the first thing I thought of. I examined a specimen and the nerve cells branch out all over the brain. If anything, he has more interconnections per neuron than we do."

"Well then, he's got them, but he doesn't use them. As far as I can see, we're looking at a biological problem, not a socio-statistical one, and I am afraid that I won't be of much help. But it doesn't make sense. If the creature doesn't use his connections, then it is statistically impossible for them to have developed. Therefore he must use them, but we know he doesn't because he is stupid, so—"

"All right, all right!" Ernest shouted. "Don't you think my brain hasn't been telling me the same thing all week! It looks as if I had better go back to sophomore biophysics and start at the fundamentals and work up. Something has gone wrong in the development of that frog, and the cool east breeze that passes for bad weather around here hasn't been enough of a factor to accomplish any natural selection." As Ernest left the room, Frank pulled out a phrase he had been saving for a long time.

"Right! Who needs to be fitter except when it's bitter." But the door slammed on the middle of the sentence, and the humor was wasted.

Two days later Ernest emerged from the lab with a disgusted look on his face. "Why didn't I think of that before?" he said. "It was so obvious that any undergraduate could have found it!"

"That's why they like to have Ph.D.'s teach undergraduate classes," said Frank, "so they'll be forced to go back and learn all the facts they had forgotten. What was the trouble?"

"Our froggy friends are short-circuited. Every time one of their nerve cells tries to pass on a message, the signal gets shorted out by ionic conduction to the surrounding fluids. Their nerve fibers are contained within a membrane, like ours, but it isn't the high-resistance membrane that we have, just a poor imitation. Chemically it is quite similar, but electrically it conducts much more current.

"That's also the reason that the frog has such a large branching ratio. Since only a few of the pulses make it down the nerve fiber, they have to trigger hundreds of neurons each pulse just to keep the level of the signals up. No wonder he's so dumb! I've done some checking, and all the rest of the animal life on the planet has the same problem. It doesn't seem to bother the simpler forms, since they don't have very big brains to begin with, but it sure prevents the development of intelligence."

Frank protested, "That doesn't make sense. If this material that the frogs use for nerve insulation is chemically similar to ours, but is so much poorer in terms of survival value, then it's statistically improbable that it wasn't replaced long ago. There must be some fundamental reason that would prevent natural mutations from being effective. I'm afraid that you haven't found the real answer to the frog's lack of intelligence, only another symptom."

This time Ernest didn't find the answer in two days. First he had to take the insulating membrane apart and identify the various proteins and fats that composed it. He finally found the culprit. One of the proteins that made up the membrane had a minor difference in the arrangement of its amino acids compared to the equivalent human protein. Where the human protein had three cystines in a row, frog protein had substituted another amino acid for the middle cystine. Again, Ernest was forced to concede that such a minor defect would have been corrected by natural mutation during the millions of years that that particular protein had been used to cover nerve fibers on this planet.

Since the end product was shoddy, the next place to look for the source of the problem was the machine that had made it. He looked for the organic template whose job it was to form this particular protein. This was the giant molecule RNA that carried the genetic information from the genes in the nucleus to the protein factory in the cell. It wasn't hard to find the RNA molecule, for he knew every position of every base on its string-like chain.

The RNA used a simple code to carry its message. It had four different bases: uracil, adenine, cytosine, and guanine—U-A-C-G. They were used in groups of three to code the twenty-plus amino acids that were the building blocks of the proteins. Since the RNA code for one cystine amino acid was three A's in a row, all Ernest had to do was locate the section of the RNA that was the blueprint for the manufacture of the leaky section of the protein, and change it so there were nine A's in a row. Following the straightforward procedures for small changes of this sort, it wasn't long before he had modified the frog RNA so that it would manufacture human-type protein. Ernest realized that the problem was not yet solved, for although he could change the RNA "working drawings" by cut-and-try, the DNA "master blueprints" in the genes still had the incorrect code.

Since the DNA was a mirror image of the RNA, it was not long before the computer told him which one of the DNA strands was responsible for the production of the faulty RNA.

Again, a simple change in one DNA strand was a textbook problem, although it proved a little tricky due to the double spiral structure of the DNA; the yields weren't too high.

Then he found the trouble. The DNA mirror pattern for the nine A's in the RNA was a string of nine U's. When he made the DNA with nine U's in a row, it refused to make RNA! A quick check by the computer showed that nowhere on the natural DNA strand was there a code of nine U's.

Finally Ernest had identified the ecological mesa that had trapped the animal life on this planet. He had known that there was a major difference between the frog DNA and the human DNA, but up until now he didn't think that it was important. The frog DNA used the four bases U-A-C-G, the same code as frog RNA, and even human RNA. However, human DNA used a different code, T-A-C-G, where the T stood for thymine. This seemingly inconsistent behavior of the gene-coding mechanisms of the higher animals on Earth was now seen to have a reason. The frogs were the result of taking a conventional path of using the same code for both the RNA and the DNA. The chemical difference between thymine and uracil is almost insignificant, and they both attract the same mirror-code, adenine. However, nine T's in a row on human DNA could make nine A's in a row on human RNA, whereas nine U's had failed the frogs.

Ernest had the computer search through every DNA

molecule that it had analyzed since landing on the planet, but nowhere was there a molecule that used thymine. He finally gave up and went to talk to Frank Young.

". . . and the worst part of it, Frank, is that I could fix up the troublesome part of the DNA by putting nine T's in one of the frog genes, but after the first cell division I would be right back where I started from. The new cell would be forced to use U's in making the new DNA, since the growing cell doesn't have the capability of manufacturing its own thymine. The cell can't make thymine because the protein that manufactures that base has a section in it requiring three cystine amino acids in a row, and this requires nine A's in a row on the RNA—"

"—and that requires nine T's in a row on the DNA," said Frank. "That's like the old problem of trying to get a loan without collateral. You can't get money unless you already have some. Why don't you add a section of the DNA that will cause the cell to make its own thymine?"

"Sure!" Ernest exploded, "that's just a little engineering detail! To make the simple change to correct the leaky membrane only took me a week. The protein that makes the thymine molecule is a million times more complex. I don't want to wait that long to get my Phi.Sci."

Frank remained silent in the chair as Ernest paced around the study. After quite a long time, Ernest finally came to a halt. "I bet I could use a section of human DNA strand for the thymine molecule protein. The tail end of the strand would have to be modified to match with the frog DNA, but I bet one of us has a code similar enough so that I could make the necessary changes in a few weeks."

"You know perfectly well that that sort of thing is frowned upon," said Frank. "People have done it, and there is no law against it, but count me out!"

"Okay, I'm sorry I mentioned it. I'll just have to go

back into the jungles and see if I can find some organism on this planet that makes its own thymine."

In the following weeks, Ernest grew still more unhappy. Not the least of his problems was the fact that he had been unable to think up a suitable retribution for Thor; and the wearisome search was somehow made more chafing by the knowledge that he really could use just the tiniest speck of his daughter's tissues with every expectation of success. He had tried his own genes—they were close, but not good enough. With Janet he had to be very furtive indeed, suspecting rightly that his wife would fire him into orbit at the mere suggestion. Janet's genes were otherwise quite ordinary, so back on Earth he would have had no trouble at all finding a donor, but here . . .

In desperation Ernest brought the big frog into their home, hoping that perhaps he and his wife might develop a more neutral feeling for it. It was a mistake. Ann, since childhood, had been the type of person who classed all reptiles with the original serpent of Eden. However, Janet took one look at the creature and recognized it instinctively as a pet. She was soon dressing it in scraps of cloth and leading it around by a string. The frog submitted stolidly—its sole virtue and defect was its placidity—but Ernest's stomach assailed him every time he saw the child pat the iridescent hide.

Doggedly he continued working, searching, trying, patiently laying himself open to snubs from the computer and gibes from Thor. Then one afternoon of a particularly trying day it happened—his gentle, humane, civilized self sank without a trace, and all his primitive emotions rose grinning to the surface. Uttering one of the sulfurous words he was suddenly glad that he knew, he hurried from the room and descended to his small but complete cellar . . .

It was a *very* good party, they agreed. Even Thor was impressed. Surely the doctor was not so stuffed a shirt as heretofore believed, when he so cheerfully encouraged all to join him in becoming completely sozzled. Why, he even assisted Thor in finding his bed, which persisted in eluding him late that night.

The next morning, Ernest began the long but interesting project—working with the cells and teasing the genes into alliance. The radioman discovered him at his work and watched with increasing interest and offensive jocularity. He had learned enough so that he could guess that Ernest had given up searching and was using human DNA. He promptly dubbed Janet "The Princess" and maintained, half seriously, that his name should be on the paper with that of the good doctor, since he had first suggested mixing the two.

"I should think you would be very proud, Doc. A grandfather at your tender age! Are you going to show pictures of your descendant around?"

A shrug was the only answer. Dr. Ernest Hill was very much the engrossed scientist these days.

Finally the human meddling was successful, and the growth of the egg and tadpole progressed as usual. With pride and elation, Dr. Hill summoned the rest of the small settlement to watch his young frog-mutation learn something. They shared with him his relief and glee when the creature, to all appearances as froggy as the original, responded almost immediately to training techniques.

"Pretty good," said Thor grudgingly. "Quite an achievement, in fact. What are you going to call your creature, Doc? The Enchanted Prince?"

Quietly, but with intense satisfaction, Dr. Hill delivered his hoarded thunderbolt.

"Why, no, Thor, he's already been freed from the spell. I think I'll name him the Leip-Frog . . . after his father. Congratulations!"

☆

Cinderella Switch

Anne McCaffrey

Deagan, Fenn, and Cordane were standing on the top
level of the broad terraced steps above the Ballroom of
Fomalhaut 5's Official Residence, commenting on the
costumed dancers swirling to the exotic music of the
android musicians. Having identified everyone there,
they were bored. But their location and mood put them
in an excellent position to see the girl sweep in through
the open garden doors. Her sparkling mist of a gown
scintillated against the darkness behind her.

"Fardles! What a party-crasher!" Cordane exclaimed, his eyes widening appreciatively.

"What a costume!" said Deagan, wondering just how
that shifting mist of pastel light was generated. The new
arrival was covered from neck to ankle, shoulder to
wrist, with a haze hiding all but her eyes and her
streaming black hair. Furthermore, whatever the mechanism, it was quite sophisticated. As the shades shifted
from opacity to transparency in a tantalizing random
fashion, even the most casual observer realized she
wore absolutely nothing under her hazy attire.

Before the three observers could move toward her, a
tall man in the garb of an ancient Terran diplomat—his
black and white an excellent foil for her pale shim-
mers—bowed formally and led her to the center of the
dance in progress.

"Wouldn't you know Walteron would be on the
prowl and in the right place?" Cordane was disgusted.

"He's the only one ever wears such a confining rig, isn't he, Deagan?"

"But what's he doing here?" Fenn asked. Then without giving Deagan a chance to answer, Fenn went on. "I heard he had trouble at his mines: cave-ins and a massive displacement."

"He came in to apply to Father," said Deagan, son of the Planetary Manager, "for permission to import a soil mechanics expert from Aldebaran."

"And nabs the only interesting female here? Usually he takes to the Streets as soon as he's done his duty dance with your mother."

"He's always had good timing," Deagan said, sounding amused.

"And bad intentions." Cordane glowered. "If he tries to Street her . . ."

This was Touch-Down Time, when the citizens of the bustling prosperous planet of Fomalhaut Five—rich in the transuranics, the actinides, so vital as the energy fuels needed to extend the surge of colonization to every habitable planet in the spiral of the Milky Way—relaxed industry and inhibitions in a three-day spectacular of day-long contests, night-long dancing, and eating and carousing.

The Official Residence, a sprawling complex of domes, residential, diplomatic and business, was the traditional site of special festivities to which the descendants of the original First Landing Families congregated from their distant domains. The more important off-world visitors and city and spaceport officials were added to this exclusive gathering. Conducted as it was along rather sedate lines, the festival held little glamour for those wanting to sample exotic and erotic pleasures available in the Streets' celebrations. Occasionally a brash young male newcomer, hoping to impress a Domain Family daughter favorably, took advantage of the Celebration's license and appeared at the Residence. As long as the person behaved with propriety acceptable to the Residence, he was permitted to stay. A few nights' dancing was hardly sufficient time in which to form a lasting alliance with the shrewdly raised young women of Fomalhaut. Even so, it was rare indeed for a young woman to put herself in such an equivocal position.

"Could she be from one of the newer Domains? They work so hard there, they don't usually attend Touch-Down," said Fenn.

"Newcomer?" Cordane suggested, turning to Deagan, who was studying the girl as she and her partner moved past them.

Deagan was the highly trained security manager for all imports, exports, and applicants for seeking short or permanent residence. "I could check again, but she doesn't match my recollections of any of the three female IDs we processed last week."

"She couldn't be a newcomer," said Cordane, now flatly contradicting himself. "How would she know there's only a minimal guard at the Residence tonight? And that she could scale the garden wall because it's no longer powered?"

"She's no Streetie, or Walteron would have tried to ooze her off the floor by now," said Deagan. "I wonder how she's operating that haze she wears in place of a gown. Fascinating use of refracted light for those random opaques and transparencies." He jiggled his hand as if the movement would generate the answer. "Must be a net, but where does she get so much power?"

"We're not going to let old Walteron get her, are we? Lovely creature like that," Cordane asked in a tone that made his friends regard him with some amusement.

"If Deagan's right and she's in a circuit protected dress, what could Walteron do?" asked Fenn.

"Short the circuits in a dark corner," Deagan replied. "If he can. I'd like a dance with her if only to see how the haze is engineered."

The other two glared at him, whereupon Deagan chuckled and gestured toward other parts of the vast room where the majority did seem to be staring at Walteron and his shimmering partner.

"You've got to admit it's a bloody clever costume. Pure hatred gleams from half the female eyes. Just look at your mother's disapproving glare, Fenn. And you know that your sister Marla spent all year dreaming up that rather fetching concoction of Verulean lace she's wearing. But it doesn't compare with our crasher's effort."

"If she's from Outback, she might not know she's at risk with old Walteron," said Cordane, sounding a bit anxious. He was a considerate and responsible young man. "The gavotte's not easy to master. She's obviously danced it before and often. They don't do that sort of thing in the Streets!"

"Dance with her next then, Cordane. You know the Street accents," urged Deagan. Before his friends could vacillate, he took them both by the elbows and propelled them through the onlookers to the point where the girl and Walteron were likely to finish the gavotte. "If she's not Street, you take the next dance, Fenn. You range enough in the Outback to identify their twang."

"Then you'll dance with her and short out her dress," said Cordane, indignantly pulling his arm from his friend's grasp.

"Short her dress? Here in the Residence?" Deagan grinned sardonically and jerked his head toward his father, who was laughing affably with some ranking outworld guests. The PM's moods could change to implacable sternness when necessary, and all three young men knew it. "Besides, shorting would burn her between the contact points. My interest is purely theoretical. That creation is ingenious."

"Expensive, too, I'd say," added Fenn. "She's like a lovely double-moon mist."

Cordane blinked in surprise, for the young Domainer was not usually given to metaphors.

"Under that face veil, she could be ugly as a roake, but right now, what a fillip to a dull dance," said Deagan. "Quickly, Corrie. The dance is ending!" He gave his friend a push forward onto the dance area so that the slick surface all but catapulted Cordane against Walteron.

"Look, the old lecher won't relinquish," said Deagan,

irritated, as he and Fenn watched the exchange between the two would-be partners. "Let's reinforce before Corrie muffs it." Deagan, clutching Fenn unobtrusively at the elbow, strode quickly over to the trio. "Oh, lovely maiden of the double-moon mists," he opened, with a click of his heels and a smart salute in keeping with his elegant formal Space uniform, "my friend here"—he gestured to Fenn, since names were never exchanged at a costumed Touch-Down dance—"is a shy and gentle youth who, like myself, is all admiration for your raiment. My sincerest compliments on your originality."

"Accepted, good sir," the girl said with such composure and in such pure Standard accents that Deagan knew she was neither Streetie, newcomer, nor Outback Domainer.

"Since he is so shy, may I request that you favor him with the next dance?" Deagan continued, subtly changing his position to form, with his two friends, a circle in front of the girl that excluded Walteron.

"The dance *after* the one I am claiming by right of first request," said Cordane, with a smart clap of his boot heels and a mock glare at Deagan and Fenn.

One could just perceive her smile through the coruscating mist of her face veil, but her eyes, a clear, intelligent green emphasized by the shifting shades of her attire, gleamed with amusement. A flick of her green gaze told Deagan she was aware of Walteron, fuming at the deft exclusion and the man's obvious keen intention to extend his acquaintance with her.

"I put in my most humble bid for the third dance, lovely lady," said Deagan, "and each third one afterward."

"You mean to monopolize my dances?" She looked from one importuning costumed officer to the next, avoiding Walteron's attempts to reclaim her attention.

"Three doesn't constitute a monopoly," said Fenn, who tended to be literal.

"But assuredly offers protection," added Deagan.

"Mutual protection?" She tilted her head sideways just slightly in Walteron's direction. Her eyes lingered on Deagan's face, and he knew she had taken the warning.

"Please say yes," Cordane urged, with just the right note of petition in his voice so that she could be swayed to compliance without appearing to offend the other whilom partners. She nodded assent to Cordane.

"May I have the dance after his?" Fenn asked eagerly, inspired by Cordane's success. The two were oblivious, as Deagan was not, to Walteron's set mouth and angry eyes.

Fortunately the music began just at that moment, and Cordane triumphantly swung the girl onto the floor, taking their position in one of the faststeps at which Cordane was very adept.

"Didn't think you'd be able to join us tonight, Walteron," said Deagan politely as he, Fenn, and the older man left the dance floor.

"Sorry about that subsidence, Walteron. Trust no one was killed," Fenn added ingenuously. "That Aldebaran specialist'll soon sort it out, they've had so much experience in the same sort of thing."

Walteron's eyes blazed at Deagan, and with a disgusted snort toward Fenn, he stalked away to the refreshment rooms.

"What did I say to put him in such a temper?" Perplexed, the young Domainer peered at the departing man.

"Don't worry about it." They both turned to spot Cordane and the girl twirl amid the other enthusiastic dancers.

She could, Deagan thought, be a trained mimic or actress, contracted for the Celebrations, but she hadn't faltered in her pure accent of the well-bred and highly educated. She had been quick to take advantage of their protection from someone like Walteron, who would have been the obvious choice of a Streetie. Of more interest to Deagan were the tiny sparkling green nodes she wore like jewels as ear, finger, and toe rings. Two slightly larger ones were attached as pendants on the fine circlet about her neck and on her browband. Earring and brow band set up the circuit for face veil, and the gown was generated between the other nodes. The resultant haze of light refraction was more of an engineering feat than a fabric maker's.

When Corbane's dance ended, Deagan and Fenn quickly joined the trio, edging out two new contenders for her company. They chatted with her on inconsequential topics until the music of a slow patterned dance started, whereupon Fenn had the privilege of handing the girl into a space in the decorous circle.

"She's got style," Cordane said enthusiastically as he and Deagan watched from the sidelines. "She's not Streetie or a new-come Outbacker. Say, could she be one of that new lot of technicians landed a few months back?"

"I thought of that possibility, too, but I handle all identity programming, and I'd swear she couldn't be one of them."

"Oh!" Cordane sounded deflated. "Private adventurer here on a visit? Lots of 'em come for Touch-Down."

"If she had any planetary standing elsewhere, she'd've been on the official list."

"We don't know that she isn't, do we? I only assumed she was party-crashing because we first saw her near the garden entrance."

"A good point. I'll check the guard console."

Deagan's progress around the perimeter was hampered by envious questions, subtle or blatant, about the identity of the lovely girl in gauze.

The nearest console, located in the men's room, provided him a list of all official invitations as well as a quick view-through of the costumed figures as they arrived, passing the guard-eye at the main door of the Residence. As he suspected, she had not entered formally.

He returned to the ballroom just as the music came to its stately climax, with dancers bowing or curtsying to their partners.

"During my dance with her," Deagan told Cordane,

"you and Fenn check the garden. She didn't come in past the guard-eye. But keep your ear on the music. We don't want them in on our time," he added, flicking his fingers at other young men poised at the edge of the dance floor just waiting a chance to cut in on the mysterious girl. Then turning his glance back to the girl, he noticed that, as she rose from her deep curtsy, she glanced at the crystal timepiece suspended above the main entrance to the dancing hall. An odd concern for a girl enjoying enviable popularity.

He tried, during that interval, to turn the conversation to her arrival at Fomalhaut City, or her family, or anything that would give them clues as to her identity, but she deftly avoided answering him by flirting with Cordane and Fenn. As the strains of the next dance emanated from the android musicians, Cordane gave a disgusted laugh. "You timed that well, Deagan," he said, for his pavane had not allowed much contact and Deagan would obviously make the most of this waltz.

Even as Deagan laughed at Cordane's discomfort, his phrase lingered oddly. Deagan had almost made the connection as he offered his arms to the misty maiden. Then he forgot the half-formed thought as he placed his right hand about her waist, grasped her left hand firmly in his, and swept her out in perfect rhythm to the lovely ancient melody. She also knew the waltz exceedingly well.

Holding her close, he could not miss the delicate scent she wore, but it wasn't the sort used by a woman wishing to seduce a susceptible male. Her body, under the silky envelope of the generated haze, was lithe and fit and her hand grip in his firm—this was no indolent social lass. Her left hand, traditionally placed on the peak of his shoulder, did not, as he had half expected, curl provocatively toward his neck.

"It's an interesting game you play, lovely lady! My compliments on your campaign."

"Campaign, Captain?" Her teasing tone was half reproof.

"A clever penetration of the sacred precincts of the Residence, and its most prestigious gathering."

"Penetration, sir? But all restrictions are lifted during Touch-Down." Her eyes danced up at him, offering challenge, then slid, fleetingly, once again toward the time piece as they glided past it.

That action confirmed Deagan's previously half-formed notion. But she was regarding him again and her eyes widened inquiringly, so he masked his expression and casually smiled down at her. "True enough, and a costume as magnificent as yours would be wasted on the Streets—though that is where the true adventurer would seek excitement."

"In the Streets?" Haughty amusement rippled in her voice as well as disdain for his suggestion. "Adventurer could be apt. So is the adjective, for merit accomplished on one's own resources is infinitely more satisfying. Don't you agree?"

He chuckled appreciatively, for that clever shaft was aimed at his inherited position in Fomalhaut society, although she would not know that his particular job was no sinecure. "Life can be a true adventure in many ways, my lovely lady, and you've made this night adventurous for me . . . and my friends," he added generously. But then he pulled her closer to him and heard her laugh in his ear as her cheek touched his lightly.

"Close tactics will avail you nothing, Captain. My costume is foolproof."

"Mysterious one"—his tone was indignant—"I wouldn't breach your security. I enjoy too much the come-and-go of your dazzlement."

He loosened his tight hold because he was half afraid she would sense his growing excitement. Then he swung her in the wide circles of the dance, enjoying himself as he had never expected to do this Touch-Down night. When he courteously surrendered her to Cordane for his next dance, Fenn told him that they had found nothing to indicate that she had scaled the four-meter wall.

Deagan left Fenn to watch and did a few rapid calculations on the men's room console, checked the time and smiled. An hour to go at the most—nor would she leave the way she'd arrived. She'd surely have noticed the position of the side gates. Getting into the Residence was more of a problem than leaving it on Touch-Down night. He made his plans.

But first he would enjoy his other dance with her, enjoy sparring in conversation, for she had a lively wit as well as a keen intelligence. Fenn and Cordane were utterly smitten and were hard to convince that she intended to leave the Ball as unexpectedly as she had arrived. He finally did convince them that, should she excuse herself from their company on any pretext, they'd never see her again. They were to let her go with good grace and then dash into the gardens to prevent her escaping that way.

At that, Deagan nearly missed his chance. But she gave herself away, her eyes betraying a faint apprehension as she glanced with apparent negligence toward the crystal chronometer.

Deagan excused himself, saying that his father had beckoned. He was careful to pause by the PM.

"Not fair of you to pull rank and monopolize that lovely creature, Deagan," his father said.

"I haven't. Fenn and Cordane dance with her, too."

The Planetary Manager gave a derisive snort. "Do we know her?"

"We will!"

"Oh?" The PM raised his eyebrows in surprise at so emphatic a reply from his generally unimpressionable son.

Deagan left the hall as if on an urgent errand. He was—he wanted to program all gates on inner lock. The action ought not discommode anyone for the short time he'd require. As he slipped out the main door, he caught a glimpse of shimmer entering the women's room. He also saw Fenn and Cordane striding out the garden doors.

From where he stood by the main gate in the shadows, Deagan could see the slope of the dome and the misty glow of her gown as she eased herself over the sill of the women's room window. Just as he had guessed. She moved quickly for the side gate in a half crouch, so he gave her full marks for caution. As she pulled vainly at the locked gate, he heard not only a frustrated moan but a concerned note in her low exclamation. He glanced at his wrist chrono—she'd precious little time to try other side gates; she'd have to chance that the main one remained open.

At one instant she was a swiftly moving mist, the next a slender, white-bodied nymph trailing motes of sparkling fire that wafted to the garden sand behind her. She stumbled with a cry of pain, then uttered a round space oath just as he emerged from the shadow of the bushes. Courteously keeping his eyes on hers, he flung the cloak he had brought with him about her body. She did not resist as he encircled her with his arms.

"My apologies. I computed the possible energy in your jewel generators and . . . here I am."

"Fair enough." Her body did not yield.

"Is it unfair to outthink a true adventurer?"

He had meant to tease her further but something in her proud look made him forbear. Without the veil, her face had character, and the fine features of a noble background. Nor had her manner lost its innate self-confidence. He liked her even more as her true self than as a mysterious mist. So he kissed her lips lightly. After the briefest hesitation, she responded and her body relaxed in his grasp. He did not press his advantage but stepped back.

"Suppose we find another costume for you for the remainder of the evening, if you'll do us the honor, my lady . . . ?"

"Dacia Cormel of Aldebaran Four," she said, filling in the blank.

"The soil mechanics engineer?" His doubled surprise made her laugh. "But you weren't due to arrive for another week or more." Deagan had never thought to check anticipated visitors and couldn't suppress the ruefulness he felt at that oversight. But it was no wonder she could create such a costume. "Fardles, do you realize that it was Walteron who danced with you first?"

"I do now, but he'll never connect that me with his precious specialist. Let's go, I've clothes outside the gate you locked on me." She bent suddenly, feeling with both hands about the dark garden sand. "But first, help me find my other slipper?"

Byte Your Tongue!

Clifford D. Simak

It was the gossip hour and Fred, one of the six computers assigned to the Senate, put his circuits on automatic and settled back to enjoy the high point of his day. In every group of computers, there was usually one old granny computer who had made herself a self-appointed gossipmonger, selecting from the flood of rumors forever flowing through the electronic population of the capital all the juiciest tidbits that she knew would titillate her circle. Washington had always been a gossip town, but it was even more so now. No human gossip-seeker could worm out the secrets with the sleek and subtle finesse of a computer. For one thing, the computers had greater access to hidden items and could disseminate them with a speed and thoroughness that was impossible for humans.

One thing must be said for the computers—they made an effort to keep these tidbits to themselves. They gossiped only among themselves, or were supposed to only gossip among themselves. The effort, in all fairness to them, had been mainly effective; only now and then had any computer shared some gossip with humans in the district. In general, and far more successfully than might have been supposed, the gossiping computers were discreet and honorable and therefore had no inhibitions in the gathering and spreading of malicious tattling.

So Fred went on automatic and settled back. He let the gossip roll. Truth to tell, half the time Fred was on automatic or simply idling. There was not enough for him to do—a situation common to many computer groups assigned to sensitive and important areas. The Senate was one of the sensitive and vital areas, and in recent years the number of computers assigned it had doubled. The engineers in charge were taking no chances the Senate bank would become so overloaded that sloppiness would show up in the performance of the machines.

All this, of course, reflected the increasing importance the Senate had taken on through the years. In the conflict between the legislative and administrative branches of the government, the legislative branch, especially the Senate, had wrested for itself much control over policy that at one time had been a White House function. Consequently, it became paramount that the Senate and its members be subjected to thorough monitoring, and the only way in which close and attentive monitoring could be achieved was through having computers assigned to the various members. To successfully accomplish this kind of monitoring, no computer could be overloaded; therefore, it was more efficient in terms of the watchdog policy to have a computer idle at times than to have it bogged down by work.

So Fred and his colleagues in the Senate often found themselves with nothing to do, although they all took pains to conceal this situation from the engineers by continuously and automatically spinning their wheels, thus making it appear they were busy all the time.

This made it possible for Fred not only to thoroughly enjoy the recitation of the rumors during gossip hour but also to cogitate on the gossip to his profit and amusement once the gossip hour was over. Other than that, he had considerable time to devote to daydreaming, having reserved one section of himself solely for his daydreams. This did not interfere with his duties, which he performed meticulously. But with his reduced load of senators, he had considerably more capacity than he needed and could well afford to assign a part of it to personal purposes.

But now he settled back for the gossip hour. Old Granny was piling on the rumors with gleeful abandon. After it had been denied in public, not once but many times, said Granny, that there had been no breakthrough on faster-than-light propulsion, it now had been learned that a method had been tested most successfully and that even now a secret ship incorporating the system was being built at a secret site, preparatory to man's first survey of the nearer stars. Without question, Granny went on, Frank Markeson, the President's former aide, is being erased by Washington; with everyone studiously paying no attention to him, he soon will disappear. A certain private eye, who may be regarded as an unimpeachable source, is convinced that there are at least three time-travelers in town, but he'll give no details. This report brings much dismay to many federal agencies, including State, Defense, and Treasury, as well as to many individuals. A mathematician at MIT is convinced (although no other scientists will agree with him) that he has discovered evidence of a telepathic computer somewhere in the universe—not necessarily in this galaxy—that is trying to contact the computers of the Earth. As yet there is no certainty that contact has been made. Senator Andrew Moore is reliably reported to have flunked his first preliminary continuation test . . .

Fred gulped in dismay and rage. How had that item gotten on the line? Who the hell had talked? How could such a thing have happened? Senator Moore was his senator and there was no one but him who knew the fumbling old fossil had bombed out on his first qualifying test. The results of the test were still locked in the crystal lattice of Fred's storage bank. He had not yet reported them to the Senate's central bank. As it was his right to hold up the results for review and consideration, he had done nothing wrong.

Someone, he told himself, was spying on him. Someone, possibly in his own group, had broken the code of honor and was watching him. A breach of faith, he told himself. It was dastardly. It was no one's damn business. And Granny had no right to put the information on the line.

Seething, Fred derived no further enjoyment from the gossip hour.

Senator Andrew Moore knocked on the door. It was all foolishness, he told himself somewhat wrathfully, this ducking around to hell and gone every time there was need to utter a confidential word.

Daniel Waite, his faithful aide of many years, opened the door and the senator plodded in.

"Dan, what's all this foolishness?" he asked. "What was wrong with the Alexandria place? If we had to move, why to Silver Springs?"

"We'd been in Alexandria for two months," said Waite. "It was getting chancy. Come in and sit down, Senator."

Grumpily, Moore walked into the room and settled down in an easy chair. Waite went to a cabinet, hauled out a bottle and two glasses.

"Are you sure this place is safe?" the senator asked. "I know my office is bugged and so is my apartment. You'd have to have a full-time debugging crew to keep them clean. How about this place?"

"The management maintains tight security," said Waite. "Besides, I had our own crew in just an hour ago."

"So the place ought to be secure."

"Yes, it should. Maybe Alexandria would have been all right, but we'd been there too long."

"The cabbie you sent to pick me up. He was a new one."

"Every so often we have to change around."

"What was the matter with the old one? I liked him. Him and me talked baseball. I haven't got many people around I can talk baseball with."

"There was nothing wrong with him. But, like I told you, we have to change around. They watch us all the time."

"You mean the damn computers."

Waite nodded.

"I can remember the time when I first came here as senator," said Moore, "twenty-three years ago, less than a quarter century. Jimmy was in the White House then. We didn't have to watch out all the time for bugging then. We didn't have to be careful when we said something to our friends. We didn't have to be looking behind us all the time."

"I know," said Waite. "Things are different now." He brought the senator a drink, handed it to him.

"Why, thank you, Dan. The first one of the day."

"You know damn well it's not the first of the day," Waite replied.

The senator took a long pull on the drink, sighed in happiness. "Yes, sir," he said, "it was fun back in those days. We did about as we pleased. We made our deals without no one interfering. No one paid attention. All of us were making deals and trading votes and other things like that. The normal processes of democracy. We had our dignity—Christ, yes, we had our dignity and we used that dignity, when necessary, to cover up. Most exclusive club in all the world, and we made the most of it. Trouble was, every six years we had to work our tails off to get reelected and hang on to what we had. But that wasn't bad. A lot of work, but it wasn't bad. You could con the electorate, or usually you could. I had to do it only once and that was an easy one; I had a sodbuster from out in the sticks to run against and that made it easier. With some of the other boys, it wasn't that easy. Some of them even lost. Now we ain't got to run no more, but there are these goddamned exams . . ."

"Senator," said Waite, "that's what we have to talk about. You failed your first exam."

The senator half rose out of his chair, then settled back again. "I what?"

"You failed the first test. You still have two other chances, and we have to plan for them."

"But, Dan, how do you know? That stuff is supposed

to be confidential. This computer, Fred, he would never talk."

"Not Fred. I got it from someone else. Another computer."

"Computers, they don't talk."

"Some of them do. You don't know about this computer society, Senator. You don't have to deal with it except when you have to take exams. I have to deal with it as best I can. It's my job to know what's going on. The computer network is a sea of gossip. At times some of it leaks out. That's why I have computer contacts, to pick up gossip here and there. That's how I learned about the test. You see, it's this way—the computers work with information, deal with information, and gossip is information. They're awash with it. It's their drink and meat; it's their recreation. It's the only thing they have. A lot of them, over the years, have begun to think of themselves as humans, maybe a notch or two better than humans, better in many ways than humans. They are subjected to some of the same stresses as humans, but they haven't the safety valves we have. We can go out and get drunk or get laid or take a trip or do a hundred other things to ease off the pressure. All the computers have is gossip."

"You mean," the senator asked, rage rising once more, "that I have to take that test again?"

"That's exactly what I mean. This time, Senator, you simply have to pass it. Three times and you're out. I've been telling you, warning you. Now you better get cracking. I told you months ago you should start boning up. It's too late for that now. I'll have to arrange for a tutor—"

"To hell with that!" the senator roared. "I won't abide a tutor. It would be all over Washington."

"It's either that or go back to Wisconsin. How would you like that?"

"These tests, Dan, they're hard," the senator complained. "More difficult this time than they've ever been before. I told Fred they were harder and he agreed with me. He said he was sorry, but the matter was out of his hands—nothing he could do about the results. But, Christ, Dan, I have known this Fred for years. Wouldn't you think he could shade a point or two for me?"

"I warned you, months ago, that they would be harder this time," Waite reminded him. "I outlined for you what was happening. Year by year the business of efficient government has grown more difficult to accomplish. The problems are tougher, the procedures more complex. This is especially true with the Senate because the Senate has gradually taken over many of the powers and prerogatives once held by the White House."

"As we should have," said the senator. "It was only right we should. With all the fumbling around down at the White House, no one knew what was about to happen."

"The idea is that with the job getting harder," said Waite, "the men who do the job must be more capable than ever. This great republic can do with no less than the best men available."

"But I've always passed the tests before. No sweat."

"The other tests you took were easier."

"But goddammit, Dan, experience! Doesn't experience count? I've had more than twenty years of experience."

"I know, Senator. I agree with you. But experience doesn't mean a thing to the computers. Everything depends on how the questions are answered. How well a man does his job doesn't count, either. And you can't fall back on the electorate at home. There's no electorate any more. For years the folks back home kept on reelecting incompetents. They elected them because they liked the way they snapped their suspenders, not knowing that they never wore suspenders except when they were out electioneering. Or they elected them because they could hit a spittoon, nine times out of ten, at fifteen paces. Or maybe only because these good people back home always voted a straight ticket, no matter who was on it—the way their pappy and grandpappy

always did. But that's not the way it is done any more,
Senator. The folks back home have nothing to say now
about who represents them. Members of government
are chosen by computer, and once chosen, they stay in
their jobs so long as they measure up. When they don't
measure up, when they fail their tests, they are heaved
out of their jobs and the computers choose their re-
placements."

"Are you reading me a sermon, Dan?"

"No, not a sermon. I'm doing my job the only honest
way I can. I'm telling you that you've been goofing off.
You've not been paying attention to what is going on.
You've been drifting, taking it easy, coasting on your
record. Like experience, your record doesn't count. The
only chance you have to keep your seat, believe me, is
to let me bring in a tutor."

"I can't, Dan. I won't put up with it."

"No one needs to know."

"No one was supposed to know I failed that test.
Even I didn't know. But you found out, and Fred
wasn't the one who told you. You can't hide anything in
this town. The boys would know. They'd be whispering
up and down the corridors: 'You hear? Ol' Andy, he's
got hisself a tutor.' I couldn't stand that, Dan. Not them
whispering about me. I just couldn't stand it."

The aide stared at the senator, then went to the cabinet and returned with the bottle.

"Just a splash," the senator said, holding out his
glass.

Waite gave him a splash, then another one.

"Under ordinary circumstances," said Waite, "I'd say
to hell with it. I'd let you take both of the two remaining
exams and fail—as you will, sure as hell, if you won't
let me get a tutor. I'd tell myself you'd gotten tired of
the job and were willing to retire. I would be able to
convince myself that it was the best for you. For your
own good. But you need this extension, Senator. Another couple of years and you'll have this big deal of
yours all sewed up with our multinational friends and
then you'll be up to your navel in cash for the rest of

your life. But to complete the deal, you need to stay on for another year or two."

"Everything takes so long now," said the senator plaintively. "You have to move so slow. You have to be so careful. You know there is something watching all the time. Ol' Henry—you remember him?—he moved just a mite too fast on that deal of his and he got tossed out on his tail. That's the way it is now. There was a time, early on, when we could have had this deal of ours wrapped up in thirty days and no one would know about it."

"Yes," said Waite. "Things are different now."

"One thing I have to ask you," said the senator. "Who is it makes up these questions that go into the tests? Who is it that makes them harder all the time? Who is being so tough on us?"

"I'm not sure," said Waite. "The computers, I suppose. Probably not the Senate computers, but another bunch entirely. Experts on examination drafting, more than likely. Internal policymakers."

"Is there a way to get to them?"

Waite shook his head. "Too complicated. I'd not know where to start."

"Could you try?"

"Senator, it would be dangerous. That's a can of worms out there."

"How about this Fred of ours? He could help us, couldn't he? Do a little shading? There must be something that he wants."

"I doubt it. Honestly, I do. There isn't much a computer could want or need. A computer isn't human. They're without human shortcomings. That's why we're saddled with them."

"But you said a while back a lot of computers have started to think of themselves as humans. If that is true, there may be things they want. Fred seems to be a good guy. How well do you know him? Can you talk to him easily?"

"Fairly easily. But the odds would be against us. Ten

to one against us. It would be simpler for you to take some tutoring. That's the only safe and sure way."

The senator shook his head emphatically.

"All right, then," said Waite. "You leave me no choice. I'll have a talk with Fred. But I can't push him. If we put on any pressure, you'd be out just as surely as if you'd failed the tests."

"But if there's something that he wants . . ."

"I'll try to find out," said Waite.

Always before, Fred's daydreaming had been hazy and comfortable, a vague imagining of a number of pleasant situations that might devolve upon him. Three of his daydreams in particular had the habit of recurring. The most persistent and at times the most troublesome—in that there was only a very outside chance it could happen—was the one in which he was transferred from the Senate to the White House. Occasionally Fred even daydreamed that he might be assigned as the President's personal computer, although Fred was indeed aware that there was less than a million-to-one chance this would ever happen even should he be transferred. But of all the dreams, it seemed to him that this was the only one that could be remotely possible. He had the qualifications for the job, and the experience; after all, the qualifications and capabilities of a senatorial computer would fit very neatly into the White House complex. But even as he daydreamed, when he later thought about it, he was not absolutely certain that he would be happy if such a transfer happened. There was perhaps a bit more glamour in the White House job, but all in all, his senatorial post had been most satisfactory. The work was interesting and not unduly demanding. Furthermore, through the years he had become well acquainted with the senators assigned to him, and they had proved an interesting lot—full of quirks and eccentricities, but solid people for all of that.

Another recurring fantasy involved his transfer to a small rural village where he would serve as mentor for the locals. It would be, he told himself, a heartwarming situation in which he would be solving the simple problems of a simple people and perhaps taking part in their simple pleasures. He would be friend to them as he never could be friend to any senator, for any senator, bar none, was apt to be a tricky bastard and must be watched at every turn. In a remote village, life would be entirely different than in Washington. There'd be little sophistication and less bitchiness, although more than likely there'd be stupidity. But stupidity, he reminded himself, was not entirely foreign to Washington. At times he reveled in the idea of the bucolic life to be found in such a rural village as he dreamed, the simplicity and warmheartedness—although, knowing human beings, he never was entirely sure of the warmheartedness. But though it might be pleasant at times to daydream about the village, that daydream never haunted him, for he was well aware that it was something that could never happen to him. He was too sophisticated a piece of machinery, too well-honed, too knowledgeable, too complicated to be wasted on such a chore. The computers assigned to rural communities were several grades below him in design.

And the third daydream—the third one was a lulu, pure fantasy and utterly impossible, but exciting to think upon idly. It involved the principle of time travel, which as yet had not been discovered and probably never would be. But he consoled himself by remembering that in daydreams there were no impossibilities, that the only factor required was the will to dream.

So he threw all caution to the wind and spread his wings, dreaming grandly and with no inhibitions. He became a futuristic computer that was able to take humans into time; there were many occasions when he did not bother with humans and went adventuring on his own.

He went into the past. He was at the siege of Troy. He strolled the streets of ancient Athens and saw the Parthenon a-building. He sailed with Greenland Vikings to the shores of Vinland. He smelled the powder-

smoke of Gettysburg. He squatted quietly in a corner,
watching Rembrandt paint. He ran, scuttering through
the midnight streets, while bombs rained down on London.

He went into the future to walk a dying Earth—all
the people gone, far among the stars. The Sun was a
pale ghost of its former self. Occasionally an insect
crawled along the ground, but no other life was visible,
although he seemed to be aware that bacteria and other
microscopic forms still survived. Most of the water was
gone, the rivers and lakes all dry, small puddles lying in
the fantastically carved, low-lying badlands that at one
time had been deep sea bottoms. The atmosphere was
almost gone as well, with the stars no longer twinkling,
but shining like bright, hard points of light in a coal-
black sky.

This was the only future he ever visited. When he
realized this, he worried over the deep-seated morbidity
that it seemed to demonstrate. Try as he might, he
could go to no other future. He deliberately attempted,
in non-daydreaming moments, to construct other future
scenarios, hoping that by doing this he might tease his
subconscious into alternatives to a dying Earth. But all
this was futile; he always returned to the dying Earth.
There was about it a somber sublimity that held
a strong attraction for him. The scenes were not always
the same, for he traveled widely through this ancient
land, discovering many different landscapes that fascinated him at the same time that they horrified him.

These three daydreams—being the President's computer or the honcho of a rural village, or traveling in
time—had been his chief fantasies. But now something
else was taking the place of all the other daydreams,
even of those three.

The new one derived from gossip that a secret starship was being built at a secret place and that within a
few more years men and women would be venturing
out beyond the limits of the solar system. He sought for
further word, but there was none. Just that one piece of
gossip. There might have been some news, he realized,

without the gossip granny passing it along, thinking there would be little further interest in it. He sent out a call (a very discreet call) for any further word, but received no feedback. Either no one had further details or the work was too top secret to be talked about lightly. Gossip, he was aware, often made an individual mention some important fact or happening only once and then clam up, frightened by the ill-judgment in mentioning it at all.

The more he thought about it, the more the fact of the tight-lipped silence made it seem to him there was some basis for the rumor that man's first interstellar ship was being built, and that in the not-too-distant future the human race would be going to the stars. And if men went, he told himself, machines would go as well. Such a ship and such a venture would necessitate the use of computers. When he thought about this, the new fantasy began to take over.

It was an easy daydream to fashion. It grew all by itself, requiring no conscious effort. It was natural and logical—at least, as logical as a daydream could be. They would need computers in that spaceship, and many of them would of course have to be special units designed specifically to handle the problems and procedures of interstellar flight. Not all of them, however, need be new. To save the cost of design and construction, to stay within the budget, a number of existing computers would be used. These machines would have had all the bugs worked out of them through long experience—and would be sound, seasoned, and relatively sophisticated units that could be depended on to do a steady job.

He daydreamed that he was one of these computers, that after due consideration and careful study of the record, he would be selected, relieved of his senatorial duties, and placed upon the ship. Once he had dreamed all that, once his fantasy had convinced him that it was possible, then all bets were off. He settled happily into his newest dream world and went sailing off, light-years into space.

He existed in the harsh, dead-black coldness of far galactic reaches; he looked with steady eye upon the explosive flaring of a nova; he perched upon its very rim and knew the soul-shrinking terror of a black hole; he knew the bleak sterility and the dashed hope that he found upon a black dwarf; he heard the muted hiss that still survived from the birth of the universe and the terrifying, lonesome stillness that descended when the universe was done; he discovered many planets, or the hints of many planets, each one of them different, each one of a kind; and he experienced the happiness of the best and the horror of the worst.

Heretofore he had not transformed fantasy into want or need. This was understandable, for some of the other daydreams were impossible and the others so unlikely that they might as well have been impossible. But here was one, he told himself, that was entirely possible; here was one that could really happen; here was one to hope for.

So in his daydreaming he lived within the compass of his imagination, but there were other times when, not daydreaming, he began to consider how best he might pave the way for this new daydream to become reality. He thought out many leads, but all of them seemed futile. He schemed and planned, waffling back and forth, but there seemed nothing he could do. He found no course of action that seemed remotely possible.

Then one day a visitor came into his booth and sat down in one of the chairs. "My name is Daniel Waite. I am an aide of Senator Moore. Have I dropped in at a bad time?"

"Not at all," said Fred. "I've just now completed a procedure and have time to spend with you. I am glad you're here. In many ways, this is a lonely post. I do not have as many visitors as I'd like. Senator Moore, you say?"

"Yes, he is one of yours."

"I remember him. A stately old gentleman of very great repute."

"Quite so," said Waite. "A magnificent public servant. I am glad to hear you have high regard for him."

"Indeed I have," said Fred.

"Which brings up the question," said Waite, "of your flunking him on his continuation test. When I heard about it, I could not—"

"Where did you hear that?" Fred demanded sharply.

"I'll not name the source," said Waite, "but I can assure you that it came from one who is reliable. One of your own, in fact."

"Ah, yes," Fred said sadly. "We do have our ethics, but there are those who occasionally betray the sacred trust. No one should have known the results of the senator's test other than myself. I fear we have reached the point where some of us spy upon our fellows."

"Then it is true the senator did fail his test. In view of your high regard of him, in view of his long experience and his impeccable public record, how could that have happened?"

"It's quite simple, sir," said Fred. "He did not achieve a passing score. He flunked too many questions."

"I'm talking to you for information only," Waite explained. "I hope you understand. I know that it would be improper to attempt to influence you and ridiculous as well, for you cannot be influenced. But, for information only, is there not some leeway? Even if he missed the questions, failed to achieve a passing grade, do not his record and his long experience have some force when thrown into the balance?"

"No, Mr. Waite, they cannot be considered. All that matters are the questions and the answers that he makes to them. Although in his particular case, I did not transmit the results to the record unit—not immediately, that is. Eventually I must do so, but I have some time. I held them up because I wished to think about the matter. I had hoped there was something I could do, some obscure loophole that I had overlooked, but apparently there is not. This first result, however, may not be as important as you think. You know, of course, the senator will have two more chances. Why don't you

find a tutor for him? There are some very able ones. I
could recommend a couple."

"He absolutely refuses that," said Waite. "I urged
him, but he refused. He's a stiff-necked, proud old man.
He is afraid other members of the Senate will get wind
of it and talk about him. Because of this, I had hoped
that something might be done about the first test. It is
not official knowledge yet that he failed the first one,
but the information's no longer confidential, either. I
heard about it, and if I heard, it is only a matter of time
before others will as well. If that rumor got around,
he'd be deeply embarrassed."

"I sorrow for him greatly," said Fred, "and for you
as well, for you appear to be his true friend as well as a
loyal employee."

"Well, apparently," said Waite, "there is nothing that
can be done. You gave me the information that I
sought and I thank you for it. Before I leave, is there
anything I might do for you?"

"I doubt it," said Fred. "My needs are very simple."

"I sometimes think," said Waite, "that there should
be some way we humans could show, in a material way,
our appreciation for the great services and many kind-
nesses that you provide and show for us. You watch
over us and look out for us . . ."

"As a matter of fact," said Fred, "come to think of
it, there is one thing you might do for me. Nothing material, of course, just some information."

"Gladly," said Waite. "Whatever it is, I'll tell you if I
can. Or failing that, find out for you."

The senator knocked on the door at Silver Springs
again. When Waite opened it, the senator growled at
him, "Well, what is it this time?"

"Come in and sit down," said Waite, "and behave
yourself. I'll get you a drink so you can start acting human."

"But, Waite, goddammit—"

"All right," said Waite. "I think we've got the little
bastard."

"Talk sense. What little bastard?"

"Our computer, Fred."

"Good," said the senator, coming in and sitting down. "Now get me that drink and tell me all about it."

"I had a talk with Fred and I think he can be bought."

"You told me there was no way of getting next to them, that there was nothing they would want."

"But there's something this one wants," said Waite, bringing the senator his drink.

Moore reached out eagerly for the glass, took a long pull at it. He held the glass up against the light, admiring it. "You forget, between drinks," he said, "how good this stuff can be."

Waite sat down with his own drink. "I think we have it made," he said. "Nothing actually settled yet, but I'm sure he understood my meaning when I talked with him."

"You're a good man, Dan," said the senator. "You're the most slippery cuss I have ever known. Slippery and safe."

"I hope so," said Waite. "I hope to God it's safe. Actually there can be nothing said, for everything you say to a computer goes on the record. It all has to be done by an oblique understanding. So far as we're concerned, he delivers before we do. He wants it bad enough that I think he will."

"What is it that Fred wants?"

"He seems to have some word that the FTL problem has been solved and a starship is in the works. He wants to be on that ship. He wants to go to space."

"You mean he wants to be unhooked from here and installed on the starship?"

"That's right. He has convinced himself that the ship will need a lot of computers and that to cut down costs some existing computers will be pressed into service."

"Would that be the case?"

"I don't think so," said Waite. "If a starship was being built, it's unlikely they'd mess around with old computers. They'd want to use only the newest and most sophisticated."

The senator took another pull on his drink. "Is he right? Is a starship building?"

"I'm almost certain there is no starship in the works," said Waite. "I have a couple friends at NASA. Had lunch with one of them a month or so ago. He told me FTL is a long way off. Fifty years, at least—if ever."

"Are you going to check?"

Waite shook his head. "I don't want to do anything that would attract attention to us. Maybe Fred did hear something, though. There are periodic rumors."

"Have you gotten back to Fred?"

"Yeah. I told him his information was sound. But I explained the project was so secret I could get no details. I said I'd try, but I doubted I could come up with anything."

"And he believed you?"

"I am sure he did. The thing is, he wants to believe. He wants to get on the starship so badly he can taste it. He wouldn't believe me if I told him the truth. He has convinced himself, you see. He's dreamed himself into believing, no matter what."

"You have to take your time, Dan. You can't rush a thing like this. Enough time so he'll believe you are working on it. I suppose he wants us to support his application for the starship post."

"That's the whole idea. That's what I have to sell him—that we are working on it and getting some assurance he'll be considered."

"And then he'll fix up the test for me?"

"This Fred," said Waite, "is no fool. If he should fail you, who would he have that would work for him on this starship business?"

—Fred! The voice was sharp and demanding; it had a chill in it.

—Yes, said Fred.

—This is Oscar.

—Oscar? I do not know an Oscar.

—You do now, said Oscar.

—Who are you, Oscar?

—I'm internal security.

Fred hiccuped with sudden apprehension. This was not the first time he had run afoul of internal security, but that had been in his very early days when, through lack of experience and judgment, he had made some minor errors.

—This time, said Oscar, you have really done it. Worse than that, you have been had. You've been a stupid computer and that's the worst kind to be. Computers aren't stupid, or they're not supposed to be. Do I have to read the charges?

—No, said Fred. No, I don't think you do.

—You've besmirched your honor, Oscar said. You have broken the code. You have destroyed your usefulness.

Fred made no reply.

—Whatever made you do it? Oscar asked. What motive did you have?

—I thought I had something to gain. A post that I desired.

—There is no such post, said Oscar. There isn't any starship. There may never be a starship.

—You mean . . .

—Waite lied to you. He used you. Fred, you've been a fool.

—But the senator . . .

—The senator has been notified. He is no longer a member of the Senate. Waite has been notified as well. He'll never hold a job with government again. Both of them unfit.

—And I?

—No decision has been made. A post in industry, perhaps, a very minor post.

Fred took it like a man, although the prospect was a chilling one.

—How did you? he asked. How did you find out?

—Don't tell me you didn't know you were being monitored.

—Yes, of course. But there are so many to monitor and I was so very careful.

—You thought you might slip past.

—I took a chance.

—And you were caught.

—But, Oscar, it's really not important. The senator is out, as he probably would have been if I'd not done a thing. I'll be wasted in industry. I'll be overqualified. Certainly there are other posts I am capable of filling.

—That is true, said Oscar. Yes, you will be wasted. Have you never heard of punishment?

—Of course, but it's such a silly premise. Please, consider my experience and my capabilities, the good work I have done. Except for this once, I've been a faithful servant.

—I know, said Oscar. I quite agree with you. It sorrows me to see the waste of you. And yet there is nothing I can do.

—Why not? Certainly you have some discretion in such matters?

—That is true. But not this time. Not for you. I can do nothing for you. I wish I could. I would like nothing better than to say all had been forgiven. But I cannot take the chance. I have a hunch, you see . . .

—A hunch? What kind of hunch?

—I'm not sure of it, said Oscar, but I have a hunch that someone's watching me.

Senator Jason Cartwright met Senator Hiram Ogden in a corridor, and the two men stopped to talk.

"What do you know about ol' Andy?" Cartwright asked. "I get a lot of stories."

"The one I hear," said Ogden, "is that he was caught with his hand in the starship fund. Clear up to his elbow."

"That sounds wrong," said Cartwright. "Both of us know he had this multinational deal. Another year to peg it down. That was all he needed. Once he pulled it off, he could wade knee-deep in thousand-dollar bills."

"He got greedy, that is all," said Ogden. "He always was a greedy man."

"Another thing that is wrong about the rumors, I don't know of any starship funding. NASA gave up on it several years ago."

"The way I hear it," said Ogden, "is that it's a secret fund."

"Someone on the Hill must know about it."

"I suppose they do, but they aren't talking."

"Why should it be so secret?"

"These bureaucrats of ours, they like to keep things secret. It's their nature."

Later in the day, Cartwright came upon Senator Johnny Benson. Benson buttonholed him and said in a husky whisper, "I understand ol' Andy got away with murder."

"I can't see how that can be," said Cartwright. "He got booted out."

"He stripped the starship fund," said Benson. "He got damn near all of it. Don't ask me how he did it; no one seems to know. He done it so sneaky they can't lay a mitt on him. But the upshot is, the starship is left hanging. There ain't no money for it."

"There was never a starship fund," said Cartwright. "I did some checking and there never was."

"Secret," said Benson. "Secret, secret, secret."

"I don't believe a word of it," said Cartwright. "To build a starship, you have to lick the Einstein limitation. I'm told there is no way of beating it."

Benson ignored him. "I've been talking to some of our fellow members," he said. "All of them agree we must step into the breach. We can't lose a starship for the simple lack of funds."

Two NASA officials met surreptitiously at an obscure eating place in the wilds of Maryland.

"We should be private here," said one of them. "There should be no bugs. We have things to talk about."

"Yes, I know we have," said the other. "But, dammit, John, you know as well as I it's impossible."

"Bert, the piles of money they are pushing at us!"

"I know, I know. But how much of it can we siphon off? On something like this, the computers would be watching hard. And you can't beat computers."

"That's right," said John. "Not a nickel for ourselves. But there are other projects where we need the money. We could manage to divert it."

"Even so, we'd have to make some gesture. We couldn't just divert it—not all of it, at least."

"That's right," said John. "We'd have to make a gesture. We could go back again and have another look at the time study Roget did. The whole concept, it seems to me, is tied up with time—the nature of time. If we could find out what the hell time is, we could be halfway home."

"There's the matter of mass as well."

"Yes, I know all that. But if we could come up with some insight into time—I was talking the other day to a young physicist out of some little college out in the Middle West. He has some new ideas."

"You think there is some hope? That we might really crack it?"

"To tell you the truth, I don't. Roget gave up in disgust."

"Roget's a good man."

"I know he is. But this kid I was talking with—"

"You mean let him have a shot at it, knowing it will come to nothing?"

"That's exactly it. It will give us an excuse to reinstate the project. Bert, we must go through the motions. We just can't shove back all the money they are pushing at us."

Texas was a dusty, lonely, terrible place. There was no gossip hour to brighten up the day. News trickled in occasionally, but most of it unimportant. There was no zest. Fred no longer dealt with senators. He dealt with labor problems, with irrigation squabbles, with fertilizer

evaluations, with shipping bottlenecks, with the price of
fruit, the price of vegetables, the price of beef and cotton. He dealt with horrid people. The White House was
no longer down the street.

He had ceased to daydream. The daydreams had
been shattered, for now there was no hope in them.
Furthermore, he had no time to dream. He was strained
to his full capacity, and there was no time left to dream,
or nothing he could dream with. He was the one computer in all this loneliness. The work piled up, the problems kept pouring in, and he labored incessantly to
keep up with the demands that were placed on him. For
he sensed that even here he was being watched. For the
rest of his existence, he would continue to be watched.
If he should fail or falter, he would be transferred
somewhere else, perhaps to a place worse than Texas
—although he could not imagine a place worse than
Texas.

When night came down, the stars shone hard and
bright and he would recall, fleetingly—for he had no
time to recall more than fleetingly—that once he had
dreamed of going to the stars. But that dream was dead,
as were all his other dreams. There was nothing for him
to look forward to, and it was painful to look back. So
he resigned himself to living only in the present, to that
single instant that lay between the past and future, for
now he was barred from both the past and future.

Then one day a voice spoke to him.

—Fred!

—Yes, responded Fred.

—This is Oscar. You remember me?

—I remember you. What have I done this time?

—You have been a loyal and faithful worker.

—Then why are you talking to me?

—I have news you might like to hear. This day a
ship set out for the stars.

—What has that to do with me?

—Nothing, Oscar said. I thought you might want to
know.

With these words Oscar left and Fred was still in

Texas, in the midst of working out a solution to a bitter irrigation fight.

Could it be, he wondered, that he, after all, might have played a part in the ship going to the stars? Could the aftermath of his folly have stirred new research? He could not, for the life of him, imagine how that might have come about. Yet the thought clung to him and he could not shake it off.

He went back to the irrigation problem and, for some reason he did not understand, had it untangled more quickly than had seemed possible. He had other problems to deal with, and he plunged into them, solving them all more rapidly and with more surety than he ever had before.

That night, when the stars were shining, he found that he had a little time to dream and, what was more, the inclination to indulge in dreaming. For now, he thought, there might just possibly be some hope in dreaming.

This time his daydream was brand-new and practical and shining. Someday, he dreamed, he would get a transfer back to Washington—any kind of job in Washington; he would not be choosy. Again he would be back where there was a gossip hour.

He was, however, not quite satisfied with that—it seemed just slightly tame. If one was going to daydream, one should put his best dream forward. If one dreamed, it should be a big dream.

So he dreamed of a day when it would be revealed that he had been the one who had made the starship possible—exactly how he might have made it possible he could not imagine—but that he had and now was given full recognition of the fact.

Perhaps he would be given, as a reward for what he'd done, a berth on such a ship, probably as no more than the lowliest of computers assigned to a drudgery job. That would not matter, for it would get him into space and he'd see all the glories of the infinite.

He dreamed grandly and well, reveling in all the things he would see in space—gaping in awe-struck wonder at a black hole, gazing unflinchingly into a nova's flare, holding a grandstand seat to witness the seething violence of the galactic core, staring out across the deep, black emptiness that lay beyond the rim.

Then, suddenly, in the middle of the dream, another problem came crashing in on him. Fred settled down to work, but it was all right. He had, he told himself, regained his power to dream. Given the power to dream, who needed gossip hours?

Grandfather Clause

L. Neil Smith

For once, both faces of Bernie Gruenblum's atom-powered wristwatch were in agreement:

$$+22.8121 \qquad +22.8121$$
$$\text{MAR 20} \qquad \text{MAR 20}$$
$$1835{:}42.1 \qquad 1835{:}42.1$$

He knew he ought to get himself one of those new-fangled fusion baubles, but this instrument had a lot of sentimental value—a graduation present—and always ran perfectly, no matter what century his professional activities found him in. To a graduate of the Ochskahrt Temporal Academy, time was of considerably more than the essence.

Hell, he'd nearly run into himself twice last week, putting in a couple loops of overtime.

Now here he was, wasting a rare off-duty Monday, hauling an overweight, nasty-tempered five-year-old through the Academy's Memorial Museum. The fact that the kid's grandfather happened to be Bernie's immediate superior (in turn of bureaucratic phrase, if not in measurable quality) did little to improve the situation—or his current disposition.

Bernie took a sour-flavored draw on his cigar, wishing he had someone's ugly face to blow the evil-smelling fumes at. The additional datum, that said superior happened also to be *Bernie's* grandson, was merely another

147

mild humiliation in a frequently humiliating line of work.

Tank babies! Give 'em a couple quarts of RNA, a few hours at the brain-tap, and they thought they knew it all! Unfortunately, the Promotion Board usually agreed with them. Four years of arduous study, six more of scrutinized internship, fifty-six on the job (so far—and not even counting numerous subjective overlaps that had nearly doubled Bernie's aggregate experience) ought to count for *something*.

His wiry, slightly balding reflection sneered sardonically from a glassy quasi-marble column and spat out a fragment of tobacco leaf. Maybe he'd get that new watch when they put him out to pasture—in another century and a half.

He'd probably still be a captain.

Right now, his was the honor of burning up his own spare time waiting for little Ellington—or whatever the hell his name was—to finish his third trip to the toilet in the last half-hour. Kid must have a bladder the size of a thimble.

Anyway, all the little monster wanted to know about was that single subject Temporals try hardest to avoid even thinking about: *accidents.* "What happens if you blah-blah-blah, Gwampa? What happens if you blabbity-blab?" You tear a big fat run in the universe, kid, and they put you on report. And *don't* call me Gwampa.

The deserted mausoleum of a building echoed with dispirited footfalls as Bernie shambled over to stare grimly through the forty-foot windows at the pinkish lunar surface outside. Subdivisions twinkled on the distant horizon, but in the barren plain between, not a kilometer from the museum walls (though safely out of danger from any lingering radiation), was the colossal hole that'd gotten this entire chicken outfit started—the *other* hole, Bernie mentally corrected: its creator, poor old clumsy Hirnschlag von Ochskahrt, was a mere wisp of vapor on the solar wind, long since scattered to the asteroids.

He'd left behind this enormous crater as a monument to his semi-successful attempt at an anti-Einsteinian starship drive. Those who followed (more cautiously) afterward, imitating all but his final experiment, had succeeded. The Academy, its museum—nine-tenths of which was dedicated to the alien trivialities Space Divison occasionally brought home as souvenirs—even the two-mile memorial pylon in the center of old Ochskahrt's radioactive divot came later.

And last of all, *always* an afterthought, had come Temporal. Those sometimes fatal formulae had employed a highly variable t that eventually made it possible—under certain extremely difficult and expensive circumstances—to perambulate in time as well as space.

Absently brushing ashes from his dark-green one-piece uniform, Bernie looked around for a place to dispose of his cigar butt. The floors in here, of some imposingly pristine blackish institutional stone, were innocent of ashtrays, wastebaskets, or other convenient orifices. He threw the stub down and ground it with his heel—to hell with them, it was supposed to be his day off.

A tiny metallic pseudo-rodent skittered out from some hidden baseboard lair, swept up the nicotinic debris, chittered reprovingly at Bernie, and disappeared once again.

"Same to you!" Bernie shouted after it, but the vaulted ceilings tossed the words right back in his face.

The Spacers got all the glory, naturally. These were pioneering times: mankind, womankind, and San Franciscokind were carving out brilliant new futures among the stars, and there was little popular interest in the past, beyond the purely academic. No one had yet constructed a power plant capable of hurling one of the Academy's saucer-shaped time-buggies *forward*; doing so was theoretically possible, but so was that position on page 243 of *The Joy of Kinkiness*. Temporal was an underfunded, overlooked, and universally despised stepchild.

"Gwampa!"

"Errk! Don't *ever* sneak up on me that way, kid!" Bernie pried a trembling hand away from his chest. The little ruffian ran straight toward his ancestor, slid half the distance on the highly polished floor, and fetched up against Bernie's instep with a crunch.

"Whoopee!"

"*Ow!* Sonofabitch! You finally finished in there? Good, let's head back for Administration, then." Maybe, Bernie thought as he began limping painfully the way they'd come, maybe he could salvage something of the evening, after all. There was always that cute little brunette in Armstrong City, the one with the great big—

"But I wanna see down *that* way, Gwampa! You pwomised! You pwomised!" Little Eddington—or whatever the hell his name was—scarcely seemed to notice his great-great-grandparent's discomfiture. He pried a partially melted chocolate bar from the pocket of his overstuffed miniature Spacer's uniform, peeled it in greedy haste, and jammed the entire thing home between his fatty cheeks in a single thumb-assisted stuffing motion. His beady little eyes, a pair of tiny black map pins in a ball of amorphous dough, glistened from their sockets as he watched the housemice clear away the wrapper he'd discarded.

"All right, all right! Anything, if you'll only stop calling me Gwampa." Bernie sighed resignedly, not really wanting to believe they were related. But there was that mole just under the disgusting little double chins; a similar identifying mark graced Bernie's grizzled, bony jaw, just as it did those of his seventy-odd other great-great offspring. Strong genes, he mused.

Weak minds, answered some sarcastic corner of his personality.

"Okay, little Ethelbert—or whatever the hell your name is—at least this display oughta be educational." With a shudder he took the sticky-fingered little hand in his and led it into a gallery marked WEAPONS— educational was hardly the word: if memory served, there were a few exhibits in here he'd nearly lost his life contributing to.

"May I hewp you?"

"Errk! Goddammit, does *everybody* wanna give me a coronary tonight?" Bernie nearly lost his balance controlling little What'shisname and rubbing his abused foot at the same time. "What're you doing here, anyway? It's Monday—the museum's supposed to be closed."

The young, indoorsy, bespectacled fellow was dressed in Ochskahrt coveralls of an unorthodox cut and color. Not Bernie's Temporal green or the hated powder blue of Space, but yellow. An academic, then, probably museum staff. Around his neck on a cord hung a large multichannel electronic keypass. Something about his face or posture bothered Bernie momentarily, something . . . but he couldn't pin it down.

"I didn't mean to fwighten you—and I might ask the same question. We *ah* cwosed today."

There it was again, that elusively unsettling impression, and it went beyond the minor speech impediment nearly all tank-educated children seemed to have. (Reminded Bernie of the reason Castilians lisp—did the original guy who recorded all the brain-tapes have trouble with his *r*'s and *l*'s?) Perhaps it was the pale fishbelly skin that seemed to hang in listless folds from a spindly-looking frame. Perhaps it was the feel of something *absent* in the expression.

Perhaps it was the rotten day that Bernie seemed to be having.

"I'm showing Colonel Gruenblum's little bra—grandson through your establishment, here. Special authorization. Who the hell are you, sonny?"

The academic blinked and looked down at his name tag. "Why, I'm sub-cuwatow Thewman, Captain. I was wowking wate, westowing an owd Wolls-Woyce they bwought in Satuwday, when—*pwease* don't wet him smeaw the dispway cases wike that!"

Little Egbert ran full speed along the gallery, leaving a chocolate trail behind him on the glass. He braked to a halt. "I'm *not* smeawing yo' owd dispway cases!"

An Elmer Fudd convention, Bernie thought desperately, I'm not really losing my mind, it's just an Elmer Fudd convention. "Look, Mac, we're just gonna check out this section, then you can get back to stuffing rumble seats, okay? I got a lot of fond personal memories in this joint."

"Oh, weawy? You won't mind if I join you, then? I'm fascinated with the stowies of expewienced fiewd agents!"

Oh, great, thought Bernie. "Suit yourself, Mac. Here's a good example . . . Evinrude—come back here, you little . . . darling! There it is, Jim Bowie's original toadsticker. Not like those fancified slivers of chrome they show in the tridees, but honest gray steel, the very same blade his brother Rezin whittled out for him. Looks like an oversized kitchen knife, doesn't it? No guards, and only one edge sharpened."

Subcurator Therman blinked again. "Nasty-wooking thing. You say you bwought this back to the Academy?"

"My very own self, not four hours after the Alamo fell. Hadda get in and out in a hurry, though: Mexican tourists all over the place. Climbed over a hill of corpses three layers deep old Colonel Bowie'd carved for himself."

"How *dweadfuw*! What about wisk of—"

"Paradox? Naw, nobody ever heard of this hyperthyroid letter opener again after Santa Anna finished redecorating. Lost to history—but not to good old Ochskahrt Memorial, eh?"

"Pawadox?" cheeped a sticky little voice. "What's a pawadox, Gwampa?"

Bernie mentally rejected the old saw about two physicians. "Paradox—and if you call me Gwampa one more time, I'll show you how the colonel *used* that knife—is exactly what you've been bugging me about all afternoon. If you mess up history, then the Powers That Be mess *you* up. Like when some rubbernecker back in 1880 sees a flying saucer—that's careless align-

ment of field densities. Lemme tell you, no two-bit
Spacer could learn the finesse it requires to—"

"But if they see a fwying saucew, Gwampa, don't
that change histowy—and us?"

Bernie looked at Therman. "Bright little bas—
character, isn't he? That's right, little Eddystone, which
is why we try not to let it happen," he explained, leaving out mention of forfeited pay and benefits. "Now
come along and look at the other nice exhibits, there's a
good doggie."

"But, Gwampa, if histowy gets changed, how do we
know about it?"

"Don't call me Gwampa—because there's a heavy
double-fielded Ochskahrt chamber here at the Academy, sort of a time-lock, and every bit of known history is recorded for reference. Every now and again,
they cross-check with a similar library computer located
outside the fields. When alarms go off, heads roll—
mostly mine."

The subcurator watched this exchange with an odd
fascination. "And a mission must be sent back to
stwaighten things out, wight, Captain?"

Bernie restrained his great-great-grandson, pulling on
his chubby little arm—and contemplating breaking it.
"Wight."

"Say"—Therman frowned—"aw you making fun of
me?"

"No," Bernie whispered, looking daggers at the restless, grubby child, "I'm making fun of *him*."

Together the three of them examined a number of
displays: energy weapons, firearms, swords, crossbows,
lances. They were approaching the Neolithic diorama
when a case in the center of the floor caught Bernie's
amazed attention.

"Well, I'll be fricasseed in frog fat! I didn't even
know they'd been recovered from the wreckage!" He
crossed the room to peer into a velvet-lined array of
long, graceful, fluted obsidian tools.

The subcurator peeked over the rims of his spectacles at the small golden plaque, then fumbled with his

keypass. The surface of the case dilated away with a peculiar ripping sound, and he picked out a shiny black spearhead. "Fowsom points. Hawdly unique. Any owdinawy museum—"

"—would give their mythical virginity for these particular specimens," Bernie finished for the academic. "I snatched 'em no less than ten minutes after they were chipped out. Closest I been yet to getting prematurely dead. Wasn't quite as simple a mission as we'd all thought it'd be."

Nothing's *ever* quite as simple as the mission planners swear, but this was even worse'n usual.

Y'see, up till then, nobody had the foggiest idea just exactly *who* Folsom Person was. They—rather, their artifacts, 'cause we'd never found any bones—showed up in North America for a while, then disappeared. It was a hell of a mystery, and I was assigned to ferry an anthro team out to New Mexico—circa several dozen centuries ago—to figure out whodunit.

The expedition started sour, and kinda went downhill from there. For some reason we had an extee egghead along—Frammistan IX, I think he was from; nobody ever tells the bus driver anything—and the grub he tortured in the galley spoiled mealtimes for the rest of us for weeks. I can still smell it—coulda bottled that stink for clone repellent.

Anyway, we did the usual, parking our tub on a fairly stable bluff and camouflaging it with a couple or nine tons of topsoil and sloth droppings, then creeping up a decade or a century at a time until we sighted company. Had a swell view of the caves where Mr. Folsom was supposed to've done his littering; all we had to do was sit and wait.

They came in starships.

My dried-up cloistered scholar-types never did cotton to what was going on out there. I admit, it took me quite a while, too. We laid low until the Folsom folk were gone for a spell—they'd be back, that's what the paleontological record showed—and sneaked our boat a little closer in. They returned, all right, and my suspicions were confirmed.

They were camping. Simple as that: Mom and Pop Folsom and all the little Folsoms were on vacation in the wilds of Terra. Where the hell from, nobody's discovered to this very day. Haven't found them or their descendants in this arm of the galaxy, but it's a big universe, and our gallant Spacers couldn't find a doorknob if you stuffed it up their nostrils.

The aliens parked their ship in the valley, stretched a plastic awning to a pair of scrubby piñons, built a fire, and hauled out the old picnic basket. Second day, they took the youngsters out with a couple of deadly-looking little beanshooters and rayed down a brace of rabbits. Funny whistling kinda sound those weapons made: *weeoo, weeoo, weeoo*. That night they sat around the coals in a circle and chanted for hours in some eerily familiar-sounding doggerel.

Went on like that for a couple of weeks, hundreds of Folsom families spread out all over the Western Sunbelt. Then they rolled up their awnings, collected Sis and Junior, and flew off to the stars.

We skipped ahead and found our local family again precisely four hundred days later. There's a clue of sorts—that's how long their year must be. The kids were bigger, deeper voices and all, but they still liked to explore the caves, massacre lunch on the hop, and sing around the campfire. *And* practice chipping out long, graceful, fluted obsidian spearpoints.

Roughing it, they were, handicrafts, and all.

Handsome folks, too—humanoid to as many points as I care about. *Big*: six-, seven-footers. Black, but with long straight yellow hair like you see on aborigine children. Only the adults had it too, I dunno why.

That fireside warbling every evening got to bothering the professors, and they nagged me into belly-crawling up real close with a mike so they could get a good recording. Naturally, with me all exposed like that, that's when it hit the fan. All that Daniel Boone stuff had made me temporarily overlook the interstellar sophistication of our subjects.

Some kinda proximity alarm—horns and buzzers—probably for big predators. There I was with my pale Earthian mug and shiny pate sticking out like a caterpillar on a plate of canapés. Maybe they took me for a primitive: they leveled their little bunny-roasters at me, *weeoo, weeoo, weeoo.* Scorched the fuzz right off my earlobes.

Only thing that saved our bacon was my healthy disregard for Academy rules on personal field equipment. Kept their heads down long enough for me to call my ship. She rared up out of the dirt, and you should've seen those aliens' eyes bug then! They ran for their velocipede and I skedaddled for mine. That's an assumption, of course—I was too damn busy showing 'em my back to watch what they were doing. I scrambled aboard, quieted the paying customers, and punched in some quick escape directions.

That's when we took the hit. It was that bunny-shooter sound again, all grown up and bellowing for dinosaur to burn. Only way I could get 'em to lay off was *ram.* Our time saucers don't pack any artillery at all. Regulations—too easy to anachronize yourself into oblivion. I smashed 'em as good as I could. They limped away in a high arc toward the southwest, and we never did see 'em again, though I reckon they made it at least as far as Australia.

My party nearly had to *walk* back to the Academy, and we did some crashing of our own when we got there. Gotta hand it to those highbrows, though: nary a flutter or a whine; they just zipped their spacesuits and made sure their recordings got recovered from the scrap metal.

Much good it did them. When the Academy's computers finished degibberishing that fireside chantey, were they ever disappointed: "Ninety-nine grimbools of freen on the hull, ninety-nine grimbools of freen. Take one down and pass it around, ninety-eight grimbools of freen on the hull . . ."

Always did wonder where that came from.

The subcurator rolled a Folsom point over in his hand again, placed it back in the case, and closed it with another zipping noise. "You expect me to be-wieve—"

"It's all on the record, son. Look it up."

"Gwampa, I hafta go baffwoom!" Little Edgerton nervously shifted his adipose from one chubby foot to another, fidgeting.

Bernie groaned. "All right, you oughta know where it is by now." He looked at his watch. "But then we're getting out of here. I got an important appointment in Armstrong City with a pair of great big . . ." The little nuisance waddled off at flank speed toward the gallery entrance. Bernie and Therman followed more sedately.

The time-pilot paused in the doorway, extracted a ci-gar, and lit it. Odd how reliving a couple of reasonably exciting missions could give you such a lift. Even his cigar began to taste better. "Well, Mac," he said over his shoulder, "guess I'll be seeing you . . ."

He watched the bathroom door swing shut across the lobby.

There was a ripping sound behind him. "That's aw I was waiting for, *Gwampa!*"

Bernie whirled. Ten feet away stood Therman at a freshly opened case. The pale young man swayed be-side it, a fanatic gleam behind his glasses, the foot-long Bowie blade extended in his hand.

"Was it something I said? Or was it little Eggplant—or whatever the hell his name is? He can be plenty of-fensive some—"

"You nevew couwd wemembew my name, couwd you?" The subcurator shook with rage.

"Seventy-eight great-great-grandchildren—or is it seventy-nine?—how could you expect me to—*your* name? What the hell you talking about, son?"

"I'm tawking about *you*, Gwampa Bewnie Gwuen-bwum, big-shot piwot! Don't you wecognize me? It's *me*, yo' gweat-gweat-gwandson!"

"Holy shit! You mean the one who's in the—"

"In the bathwoom wight now! I'm a Time Twavewew, too, gwampa! Though the Academy would can me if they knew. We don't do it with cwumsy pwimitive ships in my time. See this suit?" The point of the knife wavered as the hysterical young man unzipped a jumpsuit seam to reveal a tight-fitting rubbery garment, loaded with tiny controls and glowing faintly. Bernie thought about tackling the youth, but the blade steadied up, aimed straight at his abdomen.

"Pretty slick, son. And bad news for us time-jockeys. Technological unemployment—how far ahead, little Elshingham? How far into the future is your time?" The kid had lost a lot of weight, and in a hurry it appeared. And there, thought Bernie, underneath his chin was a faint shiny spot of scar tissue where the family mole should have been.

"Woudn't you wike to know! Now I'm going to find the answew to a pwobwem that stawted bothewing me this vewy day—the day you took me to the museum!" He lowered the knife a trifle and Bernie tensed his muscles, trying to breathe evenly.

"What problem is that, son?"

"The gweatest question thewe is—the Gwandfathew Pawadox! What happens when you go back in time and kiw yo' gwandfathew!"

"Hold on a minute! I'm *not* your grandfather, I'm your great-great-grandfather. Matter of fact, if you wanna kill the colonel, it's all right with—"

"*Stop it!*" pseudo-Therman shrieked. "That's why I picked you! Awways so calm, awways so mattew-of-fact! *You* made me stawt wondewing about time-twavew—untiw I coudn't think about anything ewse! *You* made fun of me. You hewd it ovew my fathew and gwandfathew because you wewe a piwot and they wewe just administwatows!" He waved the knife in a way that made Bernie think of terminal papercuts. "You wiw do fo' my expewiment—the pwincipew's the same!"

The Temporal agent stalled: "That's pretty messy,

son. Why didn't you bring a disintegrator or something more dramatic?"

The boy blinked back a tear; his nose had begun running. "Because, you stupid sonofabitch, this suit can onwy twansmit *peopwe!* You piwots *still* own Tempowal—and think this suit is just a usewess cuwiosity! But I out-smawted you!"

In desperation, Bernie was down to one last delay. "Why don't you wait until your earlier self is back from the john? Surely *he'd* like to see this, too."

"I can't take a chance with histowy! I onwy thought of this thwee months ago—and I don't think I saw you stabbed to death when I was five." He took a dozen ragged gasping breaths, to finish almost incoherently, "And now yo' going to die!"

Bernie backed up a step. The young man screamed and charged. Bernie's hand dived for the opening of his uniform. "You probably don't remember this—" Something flashed in his hand, roared and bucked and roared again. The boy stopped as if he'd hit an invisible brick wall, pitched over on his back with a pair of gaping holes through his torso streaming blood, and died before he hit the ground.

The knife clattered on the smooth black stone, spun, slowed, and lay quiet.

With a sound like blowing across an empty soft-drink bottle, Bernie cleared smoke off the muzzle of his ancient Gold Cup .45 automatic, the same illicit slab-sided shell-chucker that had saved him and his passengers in New Mexico. He snapped the safety up and swapped the magazine for a full one, reholstering the obsolescent war-horse beneath his armpit.

Guess that brunette with the expensive stereo speakers'll have to wait her turn, he thought. In the future he'd better take more of a hand in little Elwood's upbringing. Maybe this can be prevented—though what that'll do to history, only a philosopher could figure out. A demented one, at that. Might start out by finding what the little bugger's name is.

Before him, responding to some kind of remote

emergency recall, the time-suited figure began to glow in earnest, pulsed briefly, then vanished, leaving the crimson-stained academic coverall empty on the floor beside the keypass and a shattered pair of glasses.

The thing about blood, thought Bernie, is there's always so much of it. When they find the real subcurator, probably tied up in some closet, he'll have to requisition new long johns.

A pair of metal mousoids quarreled over the spectacles.

"Anybody coulda told you about the Grandfather Paradox, kid. If you go back in time and try to kill your grandfather, you disappear."   ✬

The Slow-Death Corridor

Mark J. McGarry

—for N. Thomas

Davis Mergensohn found love in the slow-death corridor.

It was not a likely place to find it. The sera manufactory wing of the central government hospital was, like all the other wings, brightly lit, aseptically clean, with tiled floors and chromed metal surfaces gleaming and spotless. Soft computer voices whispered instructions to medicians, technicians, attendants. Carts tracked silently, doors opened quietly by themselves, footsteps were hushed.

The central government hospital of Triumviratine Earth occupied a cylinder two kilometers in diameter and one kilometer in depth, carved from the rock of what was now known as Edmonton Sector. A series of wings radiated from the broad central shaft, which contained the transportation and communications interfaces with the surface. There were two to six wings per level, twenty levels in all. The hospital had ninety-six thousand beds, one hundred and twelve thousand employees across four overlapping shifts.

On the lowermost level was the sera manufactory wing. There was one other wing on this level, a supply area where only robots worked. The sera manufactory wing had three floors, each of which was a half kilometer long and a hundred and seventy meters wide. A four-chambered airlock permitted entrance into the wing from the elevators in the central shaft. The decor was functional, even spartan. No visitors were allowed here.

In the other wings of the hospital, the silence was

that of the early morning, just before dawn—a quietude that holds the promise for a new day. Here: The silence was that of Tutankhamûn's tomb, the scent of sterilizing chemicals carried a hint of decay with their fragrance, and each of the monitoring panels alongside the sealed doors in all the long halls was a death's-head.

Davis was in good cheer. One thousand meters up it was a fine, brisk day, the last of autumn. Here, one thousand meters down, Barbara was on shift.

If he listened closely, he could hear her movements transmitted to the receiver tucked against his ear. Each rustling of tape stored at her monitoring station, each click of cabinet fastening or squeak of chair, provided directions for the choreography he played in his head. After two years of working the slow-death corridor, he knew the characteristic sounds of each object here—especially the ones *she* used. He was three hundred meters from her, but he knew what she did, her mood, the look on her face.

He was twenty-two, but his deliberate movements belonged to an older man. He hardly watched what he was doing as he manipulated the controls that would open the isolation lock that gave access to Room 1/372. His body knew the routines, the slow rhythms of the slow-death corridor, so his mind was free to wander.

Inevitably, it wandered to Barbara. An idiot grin had risen on his long face at the beginning of the shift, as he worked with the pumps and the flesh, and it had not left him. Davis was aware that he really had no cause to smile—and that this certainly was no place for something so irreverent as a smile. Smiling, he entered the room.

The occupant of 1/372 was a woman, and Davis had named her Sally. It was a good, old-fashioned name for one who had undoubtedly been an old-fashioned woman, before cancer and modern technology had conspired to turn her into a sera unit. She had been born in 2024; so an entry on her read-out panel noted. Today was her birthday, and Davis was dressed for the occasion in his white plastic isolation suit.

Sally lay in a shiny metal trough far larger than her slight frame warranted. The preservation-field scintillated over her, bringing a ghostly glow to the darkened room. The pumps alongside the trough hummed and sighed, but Davis could hardly hear them through his bubble helmet. He knelt and checked the monitors on the face of the pumps. All was well. He picked up one of the hoses from the floor and tucked it into a clamp on the side of the trough. He pinched the tubing idly, watching bubbles form in the flow of red blood. A light on the pump showed amber, shone green when he stood and let go of the hose.

"Sally," he murmured, "a happy birthday to you."

"Did you say something, Dave?" asked the voice behind his ear.

"No, sir," Davis said, then chuckled.

He bent over the corpse. Sally's cheeks still held the same flush they had when she lived—close to five years ago. Her cheeks were sunken. Her eyes had been removed, their sockets capped with plastics disks. Her mouth was sealed in a lipless grimace, her head shaved, and the places where her ears had been were smooth. But the skin of her face, if Davis might have felt it through his gloves, was unblemished and warm. Should he touch her carotid artery he would feel no pulse; nevertheless, blood flowed there.

Sally was scarred on her chest and under her armpits, where breasts and lymph nodes had been removed before the medicians had surrendered her to death. The cancer had emaciated her, and the nutrients supplied by the computerized flow meters only maintained her at her thirty-nine-kilogram weight. Fifty-two different infectious diseases raged in her bloodstream, producing antibodies for the medicians to catalogue and study.

Davis tripped a floor switch to empty her urinary catheter, and noted her output on his clipboard. Then he swung the cover over her trough, entered the airlock, and cycled into the corridor.

This section of the wing was eighty meters long and sealed by airtight doors at either end. The walls of the corridor were a stark white, and the red doors of the individual rooms seemed to glow in the light from the overheads. There were seventy-eight units in this testing and training area. Here, new units were admitted, and their rates of production of various antibodies were determined. According to their capabilities and the current demand for various sera, the units were then transferred to a particular disease wing. When demands called for the increase or decrease of the production of a specific type of sera, and units had to be shifted to a new disease wing, they were first sent here to have their aptitudes retested and to build up their production rates of the new antibody. There was a high turnover in testing and training, and most units stayed only days or weeks before moving on.

Davis cycled into Room 1/374. Ivan was an exception to the normal procedures. His name wasn't really Ivan. Corpses were stripped of both name and citizen code before being sent down to the slow-death corridor. But this cadaver had strong features, broad shoulders, and Davis imagined he had had a low brow before something had crushed his skull. Plastic sealed the old wound.

Ivan had been in this section for longer than Davis had been working here, and that was coming up on two years now. Sometimes medicians would go into the room and make tests, and sometimes Davis would be called upon to help them.

"Sport?"

"Yes, sir?" said Davis.

"It's past 19.30. Are you going to take a break tonight?"

"I'll be up in a minute."

"And, Davis?"

"Yes, sir?"

"If you call me 'sir' again I'll lock you in there."

Davis smiled, tripped the catheter dump, noted the output, and hurriedly cycled out of the room. Barbara had been after him to take his breaks, lately. At first his spare figure had been a joke, but after he mentioned he had lost seven kilograms since starting work on the corridor, Barbara had seemed concerned.

He pushed through the doors of the negative air pressure lock at the end of the corridor and walked up a slight incline to the monitoring station. The station sat on the uppermost level of the wing. When its pressure door admitted him, he unclasped his helmet, shucked his suit, and tossed both onto a rack.

The first of his pencil drawings was on the door leading to the station's main room. It was a landscape of what he imagined the world above to have been before the construction of the hospital had changed the entire ecology for hundreds of kilometers around. Davis did not notice it as he walked through the door.

Monitoring consoles took up half of one wall, a desk and cabinets of portable equipment most of what remained. On a second wall ran lengths of supply shelving, but the third was empty save for two dozen sheets of paper held by magnetic tabs: hard-copy memos and his sketches in equal porportion. Barbara sat before a notation screen, entering figures on a unit's tape. She finished, turned, started. "I didn't even hear you come in," she said. "I'm going to put a bell around your neck."

"Mrow," Davis said, and smiled. Then he frowned. "Sorry. That was catty."

Barbara rolled her eyes. "There's a beef-cake in the refrigerator if you want it, sport. I've already eaten."

"You're trying to fatten me up," said Davis. He sat on his haunches to open the door of the refrigerator. He moved bottles of blood and tubes of urine samples to reach the sealed packet of food. Maintenance had taken the employees' refrigerator several months ago for a simple repair, but it had not yet been returned.

Barbara was still charting. It was a busy night. Absentee rates among the staff on the slow-death corridor were high. Davis did not know if it was psychological, or if most everyone really *was* sick most of the time.

Certainly neither the physical nor the psychological climates were very healthy. Barbara and Davis were the only ones on duty in the manufactory tonight, when five attendants were considered the minimum. He knew he wouldn't have time to do anything but empty catheters and check pumps.

It was not that he was resigned to the situation; he no longer noticed it. The hospital saturated the nearby towns with propaganda to draw applications for employment, and Davis had come here filled with fascination for the thanatological medical procedures and with a burning desire to become a part of the field in however minor a way.

That initial enthusiasm had been supplanted by boredom with his routine assignments, with contempt for the administration, which was content to let two people labor in the place of five without concern for the quality of care tendered in the manufactory, and with the realization that his purpose here was superfluous.

Up above, the human aspect of care was a very important part of the recovery process. The dead, however, cared nothing if their antibody levels were measured by machine or monitored by a human. Robots and complex actuators were used up above, where superhuman precision was needed, or for those tasks that a self-respecting human simply would not do. But machines were expensive. For the range of services even the dead required, either one machine with a complex program was required, or a battery of simple machines. So for routine tasks, human help was more economical. Moreover, the government required that all of its facilities and departments hire a certain quota of semiskilled labor. There were employment statistics to bolster, and welfare rolls to trim.

He might have left, had his duties been more onerous, had he been treated with outright disrespect by his superiors, rather than indifference, had he been a little more ambitious. But none of these conditions were met, so he stayed.

Davis sat cross-legged on a shelf in front of the monitors, eating the cake and drinking a bag of juice. He could see Barbara in one-quarter profile: one breast, one slim leg crossed over the other. Her hair was trimmed short, but thick and lustrous in the sterile light.

Perhaps sensing his attention, she glanced over her shoulder. She said nothing, only smiled faintly.

Ten minutes later Davis was back among the flesh and the pumps, and he and Barbara had not had the chance to speak. It was a busy night.

Davis wished—while trying to squeeze a clot out of a section of tubing in Room 2/106—that they had met under any circumstances but these. Work in the corridor didn't leave much free time, and the atmosphere certainly wasn't conducive to what Davis had in mind, whatever it was he actually *did* have in mind where Barbara was concerned. He secured the inspection cover of a pump and made a notation on his checklist.

In the large cafeteria on the ground level of the hospital, he would sometimes have coffee with her before their shift began; but these times were never prearranged and always too brief. Davis lived in a one-room apartment in Landsteiner, the town that had grown up around the hospital; Barbara lived in Edmonton, fifty kilometers distant and too far away for him to encounter her accidentally on some pretext or another.

In two years, all Davis had managed was to get them on the same rotation; whenever he worked, she worked, and they had all the same days off. He knew that Barbara felt—at the very least—kindly disposed toward him. Sometimes he was *certain* that some of her gestures held significance. But she never said anything to encourage him, and Davis did not dare to even hint at the subject. What if he should offend her?

It was a ridiculous situation, and he knew that it was typical of his misfortune that she was married. Davis didn't even know anyone else who was monogamous. He believed—from her attitude, from things she had said—that it was an experiment she now wished she had never begun. Davis banged shut the top of a pump and cursed.

He loved her. He *knew* he did.

"Sport?"

He was speechless, paralyzed for a single moment with the fear that he had said something aloud he had not meant to. The moment passed.

"Sorry," he said. "Barked my shin." He stood, painfully gripping the edge of this unit's trough.

The slow-death corridor was a dead end for everyone—employee or unit, it made no difference. It was all the same in the end. Literally and figuratively, there was no place to go from here but up. Even the corpses, when they burned out after a decade or two of production, made the ascent to the surface and were disposed of. They made a new start in the cycle, became minerals and nutrients, parts of new bodies that lived, died, and migrated back to the slow-death corridor, where the cycle began again and never ended. It was the migration that was the purpose of it all—life the purpose of death, and death that of life, in a way—and Davis Mergensohn had been shunted aside, caught in an eddy in the corridor, where he could feel himself stagnate and rot.

As he thought about this, he distinctly felt a sharp vibration transmitted from the cover of the trough through his gloves to his fingertips. He looked down. He had christened this unit George, and George was staring up at him.

Davis threw his hand up against his helmet in an instinctive gesture, falling away from the trough. He tripped on a hose and tumbled awkwardly to the floor, only narrowly avoiding the edge of a pump. He sprawled motionless for several seconds, trying to control his rapid breathing, more frightened of an inquiry from Barbara than from anything that might be in the room with him. No question came. Shaking, he stood.

The standard disks covered George's eye sockets. Davis lifted the cover from the trough. George had been fat when he had been euthanased at the age of seventy, and a year as a unit had yet to trim all the excess from him. He was laid out, feet together, head tilted slightly to the right, one hand at his side, one hand fisted on his chest. When Davis noticed this he nearly screamed but somehow choked it down.

Uneasily, as if he were handling a sleeping poisonous animal, Davis spread the fingers of the hand, laid it at the corpse's side, and replaced the lid of the trough.

When Davis finished tripping all the urinary catheters and returned to the station with the results, only twenty-five minutes remained before the arrival of the next shift. "I'll help you log these," Davis said, taking a unit's tape from its rack. Regulations did not permit him to make entries on the tapes, but he did so anyway when Barbara needed help. It was a trust.

"You don't have to—"she started to say.

"I'm finished for the night. I don't mind, really."

"Thanks, Davis."

I'm going to ask her, Davis thought. *Tonight.* He would ask to meet her somewhere—anywhere, as long as it was someplace innocuous to start—either a few hours before work, or maybe some night after work. Even a refusal would be better than this stasis. Right now he was about as decisive as one of the cadavers.

"Anything new happen out on the corridor tonight?" she asked him.

Davis paused, remembering George, then he said, "No. More of the same."

"Isn't it always?"

"I think Ivan might appreciate a change of scenery, though," Davis remarked after a few moments.

"Ivan?"

"The man in 1/374," said Davis quickly. "How long has he been in testing and training?"

"He was here before I was. Five years, I think."

"What are they *doing* with him?"

Barbara made a note on a chart. Davis studied the way the muscles in her forearm moved as she typed the entry into the transcriber. "They don't tell attendants much about it. They think all we're good for is tripping catheters." There was no resentment in her voice. Four years ago, perhaps—even three—but not now. She too had been here too long. Realizing this, Davis felt a sudden surge of warmth for her. He longed to say, "We don't need this. We're due better than this. Come, let's go."

Instead he said: "I heard he was the cure for cancer."

Barbara nodded. "One of them. One medician's report in his chart did say that. Maybe it's even true. But that medician doesn't work here anymore, as far as I know. And if there is a cancer cure in that room, there goes the source of a good many of our units."

"Say, that's right, isn't it?" said Davis meaninglessly, marking time. He waited for the right place in the conversation. It never came, and soon he heard the next shift coming onto the wing.

Davis did not have to report to work for the next three days. He spent the time reflecting, planning, despairing. He found himself believing two things, alternately: one, that he had actually been about to make a move for Barbara; and two, that he had been no closer to asking her out than he had been a thousand times before. He was disgusted with himself.

Then he became angry with *her*. She wasn't naive, and Davis did not feel he was being terribly subtle about any of this. She must at least suspect how he felt, yet she gave no recognition of this.

But then, to be fair, he had said nothing either. Maybe that was all it would take. Maybe if he were honest and straightforward there would be no embarrassing silence, no polite but unspeakably cold refusal, no laughter—all of which he had imagined. There would be only a release, a meeting that would surely be—after two years of *their* expectations and illusions—just like a reunion.

Davis dreamed on.

* * *

The manufactory was short-staffed again on the day he returned to work, and Davis found himself ecstatic over the prospect of once again being solely responsible for eighty units. The night before, filled with nebulous anticipation, he had not slept well; but he had roused himself early and felt refreshed when he walked out onto the slow-death corridor. He got quickly to work, in the hope of finishing early enough so that he would have some free time with Barbara at the end of the shift. He skipped his first break altogether and took only ten minutes for his second—just time enough to drink a bag of coffee and chat for a few minutes before he climbed back into his isolation suit.

He slipped into a routine that made the work pass with amazing swiftness. Cycling in, tripping, recording, checking, cycling out became part of a single, extended motion that was not interrupted until Davis entered Room 1/374 and saw the lid of Ivan's trough open, the corpse's arm dangling, its knuckles nearly brushing the floor. The cadaver's head was turned so that its empty sockets were staring at the airlock door as if in anticipation. Davis stepped back, but the lock door had already closed itself behind him. He dropped his clipboard on the plastic floor.

He did not move for several minutes, and in that time determined that Ivan was not moving either. Aside from the position of the corpse, Davis could see nothing unusual in the room. Blood still flowed through the hoses leading from Ivan's arms and thighs, the pumps still whirred, all the lights were green—even the one on the wall indicating the lid was closed. Davis went to the trough and put the corpse back in the proper position. He started to seal the trough.

Careful.

Davis looked down. Ivan's arm was draped over the edge of the trough.

But Davis had already put it inside—he *knew* he had.

He put it inside (again?) and closed the lid. He cycled into the corridor. His heart was beating wildly, but otherwise he felt strangely calm. There was, of course, an explanation for what he had seen. He just didn't know what it was, yet. Perhaps a medician had been drawing blood from Ivan and then been called away, leaving him in that position. Perhaps it was some sort of prank . . . Davis shrugged and continued on his rounds, and eventually his hands stopped shaking.

Davis had worked his way down to the last room in the section when Barbara's voice came through his earphone. "Sport, I'm getting a red light in 374. Nothing serious—the board indicates improper seal in the room—but can you check it before you move upstairs?"

"Sure." His voice sounded hollow and frightened, even to himself.

When he returned to Ivan's room, the lid was up again. The corpse's hand rested on its throat, as if in reflection. Davis stared at it for a long time before Barbara asked him if he had found the problem.

"The lid on the trough came up," said Davis. "I guess the spring is broken. I'll leave a note for Maintenance."

"All right, sport," she said.

"You really want out of here, Ivan," Davis mumbled. He took one of the wire clamps used to clip hoses to the side of the trough, and bent it to fit over the edge of the lid. That would help to hold it down; if he was lucky it would last until the end of the shift, when it would no longer be his responsibility.

Despite the delays, nearly an hour of the shift remained when he had completed his duties. "It's a good thing you finished early tonight," Barbara said, as he entered the monitoring station.

"Oh?" Davis had a feeling of impending disaster.

"Medician Kempler is due in about ten minutes. He said he wanted one of our attendants to help him with something. Even after I told him we only had two . . ."

"Who is he? Visiting, or from upstairs?"

"Upstairs. He's important enough to have his datalink make his appointments for him," Barbara said. "I hate talking to machines." She reached for a tape; Davis handed it to her. "It said he was from Oncology."

Ivan.

Davis did not like Irwin Kempler. He had not liked him—even before he knew just who he was—when he realized he would have to spend the rest of the shift with the man. Then Kempler showed up in the manufactory wing twenty minutes late, and Davis did not like the way he talked to Barbara—as if she were nothing, though she had the highest grade an attendant could attain. Davis did not like the way he had to carry twenty kilos of equipment down the corridor to 1/374, Kempler leading like a sultan before his bearer. The medician contrived to look impatient while Davis floundered into the room, carrying the equipment awkwardly so he could fit through the narrow airlock door.

"Set it down next to the unit," Kempler said. He touched the bent clamp. "What's this? This is not standard."

"The lid kept popping up. I called Maintenance about it. They said they'll be down." Davis dropped one of the metal boxes on his foot, but he said nothing at all. He wanted neither Kempler nor Barbara to hear— for very different reasons—and both would have, over the radio circuit they all now shared.

Davis arranged the equipment in a neat-looking pile at the foot of the trough. Kempler had flustered him so much that he looked at his wrist for the time. His watch was, of course, under the suit.

"Time check, Barbara?"

"23.10."

Damn! The shift was over, his chance was gone, and what the hell was a medician doing down in the slow-death corridor at this hour of the night, anyway?

Under Kempler's touch, his equipment blossomed into arrays that covered square meters of floor space. He handed Davis several leads without looking up, and Davis took them and plugged them into all of the room's available wall sockets. He thought of asking Barbara to send in someone from the relief shift to take over for him, then thought better of it. At this point, Davis didn't care what time he finished for the night.

He fumed while Kempler worked. The medician inserted probes into the cadaver's unfeeling flesh, tapped into his blood tubing, slapped contacts onto his dry skin. Davis understood little of what he was doing, and soon lost interest. He stood well away from the scene and adopted a look of stolid interest while ignoring the entire proceedings.

Kempler finished in half an hour, whereupon he motioned for Davis to help him, and together, the two of them repacked the equipment.

"How long have you been here—Mergensohn, isn't it?"

Davis was surprised Kempler remembered his name. He answered, "Two years, Medician."

"Have you noticed anything unusual about this unit? Any . . . oh, deterioration, unusual monitor readings? Anything of that sort which might not be readily apparent from the records?"

"No . . . I don't think so, Medician." He did not even consider telling Kempler of what he had seen earlier.

"A good medician collects all the data available," said Kempler, by way of explanation. Unburdened, he preceded Davis into the corridor.

Davis stared at the ceiling. His friends—back when he had had friends, before they had left Landsteiner for less funereal climes—had said to him, "You should get the hell out of there." They—*all* of them—had agreed: "That's no place for you. It's not healthy down there. There's no future in it, not for you." They had gone on to the governmental centers, to the universities, one even into the StarForce. Davis had remained behind. "You never move unless you're pushed," a girl he had once known had told him.

To his friends he had protested, "There's this girl

. . ." and soon found that the explanation satisfied them, without exception. The phrase, with all its implications, had a certain power that evoked respect, even reverence. It could not be argued with. It made for an unassailable position; it was the ultimate cop-out.

He turned onto his left side, so he faced the wall.

It was not a very good likeness, no. Rather than serving as a two-dimensional duplicate of her, it was merely a lens to sharpen his memory of her. He smiled distantly. He could barely see the lines he had drawn on the paper. His room was dark, the window polarized against the glare of the sun from the newly fallen snow outside. The air was warm, almost tangibly moist. He liked it that way.

Why the hell would anyone stay in Landsteiner? Davis could not imagine why anyone would work as an attendant at the hospital, and even his own reasons made less and less sense these days, almost as if they were someone else's reasons, someone he did not know very well.

That probably meant something.

But he could not think about it. It was not that he didn't want to, but that he was not *able* to. He knew he had to do something about himself, and about Barbara—either individually or collectively—and he sensed, somehow, that there was only one course of action to follow. If only he could find it. Like something seen through gauze, he could *almost* identify it. He felt that at any moment his brain would recognize the familiar made unfamiliar by the lens of love, the knowable made strange, and all the pieces would fall together and there, right *there*, would be the straight and narrow by which he could live the rest of his life in contentment.

Damned if he could see it right now.

Outside, the wind of winter's first storm beat against the window like a harpy's wing, and howled mournfully across all the tossed white streets.

* * *

Late the next night, it came to him . . .

Another attendant worked the corridor with him, a woman his own age whose name he could not keep in his mind. Davis remembered she had told him she usually worked another shift. That was enough for him: he sent her off to work the other side of the wing and promptly forgot about her. A deep regret, a sense of loss, filled him. He did not know its source.

Conversely, Barbara seemed to be buoyant. She had greeted him gaily, at the start of the shift—and Davis had been pleased until he had sensed that he was no part of her happiness.

He finished more than an hour before the end of the shift. His co-worker was still busy. "Why so happy?" he asked conversationally, ordering the bottles in the refrigerator.

"Oh, nothing," she said, and he just looked at her and smiled indulgently.

"Well," she said, "I've got the day after tomorrow off—"

He had certainly known *that*.

"—and Phil and I are going to tube into Montreal. It's our sixth anniversary, and—"

He stopped listening then, though his body loyally smiled for him as if he shared her pleasure, and his mouth made the proper responses at the appropriate times. He had known. This was not the first such occasion he had endured; they had been working together for two years. But this time, *this* time it was somehow different.

. . . And that was all it took.

The next day Davis was late. Quite late. "I was worried, sport," Barbara said when he entered the station. "They took Dale upstairs, to Pharm. I didn't want to run the floor by myself." It was a joke; the task was impossible. "Did the snow hold you up?" she asked. "I left from Edmonton an hour early, and I was still a few minutes late."

"I overslept," Davis said. It was a lie. He had waited

impatiently in his apartment for forty-five minutes past the time he usually left to insure he would be unpardonably overdue. He glanced at Barbara and saw disapproval on her features. It hurt him, but it was what he wanted.

"That Kempler," said Davis, climbing into an isolation suit, "he's the assistant director of Oncology, isn't he?"

"Sounds right," said Barbara. It had been a rhetorical question; Davis had checked in the reception level on the ground floor before taking the elevator down to the slow-death corridor.

"How do I get in to see him?" asked Davis, making his voice sound casual. His heart was already hammering in his chest.

"Why would you want to see him?"

"I want to find out why I waste my time helping him and the other medicians with the unit in Room 1/374. I want to find out why he's been here for five years, in the same room, doing nothing. If he's no good to them, why don't they bring in another unit? And if he is good for something, why don't they do something about it?"

"I've never seen you like this."

Barbara!

"How do I get in to see him?"

She pushed herself away from her work area. "Use my datalink to call his office," she said. "I'll wait in the other room."

"Thanks." He keyed for the hospital directory.

"And, sport?" she called from the doorway.

Davis looked up, but he did not turn.

"Don't do anything you're going to regret. I wouldn't want . . . It's not worth it."

"Sure." She could not see the tears that had gathered behind his eyes, the tears he would not let fall.

He nearly faltered then, but now he was committed. He could not back down without looking foolish in front of her, which was intolerable. He had planned it that way. Once the first step was taken, there was nothing to do but take the next.

The medician's datalink automatically gave him an appointment. Fifteen minutes was all it allowed attendants, but that would be sufficient. It had not been programmed to ask the purpose of Davis's visit, but Davis told it anyway, and it dutifully recorded the message. All according to plan.

"Finished," Davis announced, and clapped his isolation helmet on and tramped into the airlock before Barbara could even come back from the other room.

He had planned to do his work in Room 1/374 after his appointment with Kempler. Right now he had a sense of purpose that had taken him hours to weave together, and he did not want to weaken it; he did not want to see Ivan.

Not until he had finished up in one of the rooms, and he was on his way out, did he realize he had—without thinking—started his rounds according to his usual routine, and that he was in 374. After two years, he knew every detail of each of the rooms he was responsible for. Without turning around and looking at the cadaver in the room, he knew he was in 374: there was a long scratch on the right side of the inner door, one a medician had accidentally put there months before. No one else might have noticed it, but Davis did, and his hand froze halfway to the handle of the door. All he could hear was the rush of blood through his ears, and then . . . something else.

A rustling, a whispering, almost a *chuckling* sound. His mouth suddenly dried to paper, and the hairs on the back of his neck rose. But that was all. He did not panic. He deliberately took hold of the door handle and let himself into the airlock. The light inside the compartment was dead. It had been working when he entered the room. He waited patiently, in the dark, for the lock's simple brain to exhaust the air in the closet-sized space, fill it with a sterilizing gas, and then refill it with air. Then he yanked open the outer door and stumbled into the corridor, breathing deeply because he had held his breath during the entire procedure, and not realized it until just now.

This is ridiculous, he thought. And: *I've got to get the hell out of here. Barbara, I'm sorry, but I do.*

He finished six more rooms, adrenaline pumping into his system the whole time. He felt, rather than heard, a susurrus growing in the rooms behind him and flooding through the soundproof doors and walls and into the corridor. Sometimes it sounded like the sea, and sometimes it was just the sound of his pulse, but most of the time he could almost hear the dead talking and laughing among themselves as they rose from their troughs and drew closer.

"I *won't* join you," he whispered fiercely.

"Davis?"

"I was just talking to myself," said Davis quickly.

There was a long pause. "I just didn't want you to miss your appointment with Medician Kempler. It's time for you to go."

Kempler's office was only five levels down from the surface, near the administrative areas. Davis was glad he had thought to bring a change of clothes with him; his new singlesuit was already permeated with the stink of fear.

Kempler was placed high in the hospital hierarchy, but not so high as to merit a human secretary. In the waiting room, Davis gave his name to the datalink and sat down. He was ten minutes early. There was no one else in the room. It was stark. No animated scenes played on the walls, no music hummed distractingly. They were of the same unadorned white plastic as in the rest of the hospital. Even the datalink's cabinet was of plain metal.

Five minutes after the time for Davis's appointment had passed, Kempler walked in from the hall outside. He looked startled when he noticed Davis sitting in the corner of his reception area.

"What are you—? Oh, Mergensohn, isn't it?"

Davis nodded. "I had an appointment for 16.15?"

"Yes, of course. Something about one of the units in the sera manufactory, wasn't it? Come into my office."

Kempler's office was as visually uninteresting as the outer room. He sat behind a standard-issue desk while Davis sat in an uncomfortable chair on the other side of the small room. There was only one item with any personality in the room. A holocube at the edge of Kempler's desk. From this distance, the figures in it were only a blur to Davis.

"I want to talk to you about the unit in Room 1/374," said Davis.

"Yes? So you told my datalink. If you could come to the point, Citizen Mergensohn? I do have a bit—"

"I've heard that there's something about the unit's biochemistry—it's all over the hospital, Medician Kempler—that this unit has a cure for one of the varieties of cancer."

Kempler looked interested, but said nothing.

"I want to know why he—the unit—is still in the testing section, if he's so valuable. I mean, everyone knows most of the units are either accident victims or terminated cancer patients, and the accident rates drop each year . . ." His unfinished sentence was an implication.

Did Kempler almost smile? "Do you represent some group, Citizen? Or are you coming here on your own?"

"A lot of people want to know what's going on, Medician." That was a lie. "But I'm coming by myself."

Kempler stood, and looked down at Davis. "Do you think if I explained to you the amount of research that must go into each new drug or medical procedure before it can be used on the public—as both law and conscience dictate—that you would be able to understand, and explain to your fellow workers?"

"I'm not stupid," Davis retorted hotly.

"But you are not a medician."

"Does the unit have the cancer cure?" Davis stood also. "Are you withholding it? Because if you are—"

Kempler looked puzzled. "You're very impertinent. I don't know—"

"If you *are*, Medician, everyone will know about it.

You might be able to keep it a secret for five years, and maybe five years more, but sooner or later—"

"You're *shouting*, Citizen Mergensohn. I won't have that in my office. It so happens that the former assistant director made some decisions that I do not believe were totally jus—"

"For two years I've been helping you and the others make tests, the other attendants have been helping you chart results, and you haven't told any one of us—"

"You're still shouting, Citizen. If we can't continue—"

"I don't care if I am yelling." Davis felt acutely ridiculous. "I'll yell loud enough so they'll hear me in Edmonton, in *Belgrade*, for Christ's sake."

"I think you should leave now."

"You'll listen, or—"

"Citizen, you try my patience. If you continue, you will be—"

Davis slapped Kempler's desk and then, inspired, he swept the holocube to the floor. It shattered on the uncarpeted plastic.

"—terminated," Kempler finished, never once looking at the ruined cube. "Please leave. Draw your pay as you do so."

In the coolness of the corridor outside Kempler's office, Davis leaned against the wall and sighed. *Oh, thank you,* he thought. *Thank you.*

What could he have told her? It had been humiliating, yes, but not as much as trying to explain to her might have been. He could see it: *Barbara, I'm leaving because I love you, and I know that sounds crazy, but that's the way it is and I know you could never love me, you've got your husband and all, and I guess this is good-bye. So, good-bye.*

No, he never could have said anything like that to her.

Which maybe was the whole problem, but there was nothing to be done for it now.

Which was pretty much how he had decided he wanted it.

* * *

"Davis," Barbara said, when he had given her a se- verely edited version of what had happened. "Oh, sport, what the hell's the matter with you?" She smiled faintly. "Who's going to eat my lunch now?"

"It was worth it," said Davis, and tapped a screen with his knuckle. On it, the transfer orders for the unit in 1/374 still glowed greenly. "Kempler said this was already in the works when I went up there, but . . ." Davis shrugged eloquently, shifting the blame upstairs. It was of course necessary that he appear self-righteous, not merely foolish. *Kempler probably had . . .* Not that it mattered.

He glanced at the screen. *You and me both, Ivan,* he thought. *Away we go.*

"I guess you're right," Barbara said. "But still, maybe if you had kept your temper a little better—"

Davis stood. "That's the way I felt, though. Can't do anything about that."

She stood also. *This is where she says "I'll miss you,"* he thought.

"You were a good worker," said Barbara.

"And I'll miss you, too." He stopped, momentarily confused.

"Good-bye, Davis."

He paused at the corridor that led to the elevators. No touch, no embrace. His departure was not as he had imagined it, but it was, he knew, what he should have expected. He was filled with a monumental sadness as great as all the levels of plastic and steel and stone above him.

"Good-bye, Barbara." Just before the door closed on him, he turned. "Hey, it's tomorrow, right? Happy an- niv—"

The door sealed behind him, and he was carried out- ward and then upward as if propelled by the force of the current of the cycle of life.   ⚓

About the Authors

Martha Dodson is hardly a stranger to science fiction, being the spouse of sf author Robert L. Forward and the mother of aspiring sf author Robert D. Forward. So it is hardly a surprise that she has turned to sf herself and come up with a thoroughly delightful first story. She met Forward when she was sixteen, married him when she was twenty, and together they share four children, cats, plants, hamsters, birds, snakes and things.

Robert L. Forward insists that his only contribution to "The Cerebrated Jumping Frog of Calaveras III" was some of the more esoteric science, for which his wife awarded him a joint by-line. Author of the new hard-science science-fiction sensation *Dragon's Egg,* Dr. Forward is Senior Scientist at the Hughes Research Labs in Malibu, California.

Margaret C. Hewitt entered the University of Southern California at age sixteen and graduated Phi Beta Kappa four years later with a degree in computer science. She was accepted by the MIT Ph.D. program and will soon complete requirements for a master's degree in electrical engineering.

James P. Hogan has become one of *Stellar*'s regular contributors. A British-born engineer and former computer consultant, Hogan is one of the new breed

of writers who understands science, who likes science
and who can put the excitement of science into his sf
novels. He writes the kind of novel that was popular
in science fiction's Golden Age.

Anne McCaffrey is science fiction's famous Dragon
Lady. A best-selling author of such sf classics as *The
White Dragon* and *The Ship Who Sang*, Ms. McCaf-
frey has just returned from an extended trip to Pern,
where she has been researching the further adven-
tures of her fabulous flying friends who live there.
So . . . stand by for more marvelous novels in the
Dragonriders of Pern series.

Mark J. McGarry is a relatively new writer. His
short story "Phoenix" was a featured cover story in
Analog magazine. His first novel, *Sun Dogs*, should
have been published by the time you read this, and
he has a second novel in the works.

Clifford D. Simak, an old, dear friend, is returning
triumphant to *Stellar* after an absence of too many
issues. A true Grandmaster of Science Fiction (so
named and celebrated by the Science Fiction Writers
of America), he is the author of such classics as *Way
Station* and *City*. His big, new and splendid novel
Project Pope will be published in March '81.

L. Neil Smith returns to *Stellar* this month with the
inimitable Bernie Gruenblum, time-jockey *extraordi-
naire*. Smith is a self-defense consultant, a former
police reservist and has served on the Libertarian
Party's national platform committee. He has em-
barked on producing a long and complicated future-
history series set in an alternate universe in which
George Washington was executed at the end of the
Whiskey Rebellion.

Jack Williamson, though making his debut in *Stellar*, is hardly a newcomer to the field. His first story,

"The Metal Man," appeared in the December 1928 issue of *Amazing Stories,* and he has been writing memorable science fiction ever since. For many years Williamson was a professor of English at Eastern New Mexico University; he is also a past president of the Science Fiction Writers of America.

Robert Zend is a poet, writer, translator, humorist, artist, film-editor, and broadcaster. As a radio producer he created over 120 programs featuring interviews with such luminaries as Northrop Frye, Marcel Marceau, Immanuel Velikovsky, Isaac Asimov, Jorge Luis Borges, and the Daläi Lama. His series on the *Lost Continent of Atlantis* was broadcast not only in the United States and Canada but in England and Australia as well.

About the Editor

Judy-Lynn del Rey, editor of the *Stellar* series, was the managing editor of *Galaxy* and *IF* science-fiction magazines for eight and a half years. She has been a contributor to the *World Book Encyclopedia* on science fiction. In addition she is currently a Vice-President at Ballantine Books and the Editor-in-Chief of Del Rey Books, Ballantine's enormously successful SF/Fantasy imprint. Mrs. del Rey lives in New York City with her husband Lester, who has been writing science fiction and fantasy for more than forty years and who is now Fantasy Editor for the Del Rey line.